PRAISE FOR

BAREFOOT DREAMS OF PETRA LUNA

- ◆ A 2022 Pura Belpré Honor Book
- ◆ An ALA Notable Children's Book
- ◆ New York Public Library Best Book of 2021
- ◆ A Texas Bluebonnet Master List Selection
- ◆ NPR Best Book of 2021

★ "Dobbs's wrenching debut, about family, loss, and finding the strength to carry on, illuminates the harsh realities of war, the heartbreaking disparities between the poor and the rich, and the racism faced by Petra and her family. Readers will love Petra, who is as strong as the black-coal rock she carries with her and as beautiful as the diamond hidden within it."

—*Booklist*, Starred Review

★ "With vivid and poetic imagery and artfully balanced narrative tension, Dobbs's assured writing blazes bright, gripping readers until the novel's last page."

—*Publishers Weekly*, Starred Review

"Viscerally relevant to contemporary readers."

—*The Bulletin of the Center for Children's Books*

"The parallels between past and present government corruption and violence make this historical fiction that is as relevant as ever...A timeless and timely tale of one girl's journey to save her family and discover herself."

—*Kirkus Reviews*

"This beautifully written and exciting story of a family fleeing during the Mexican revolution offers a new perspective in historical fiction."

—*School Library Journal*

"*Barefoot Dreams of Petra Luna* will draw you in with its raw, evocative setting, and Petra herself will win your heart with her courage, resourcefulness, and unwavering love for her family. Lyrical, heartfelt, and deeply authentic, this book will stay on your mind long after you've read the last page."

—J. Anderson Coats, award-winning author of
The Many Reflections of Miss Jane Deming

"What hunger would you endure, what history would you sacrifice, what hazards would you brave to lead your family through a war? Petra Luna's incredible odyssey in pursuit of her 'barefoot dreams' is as vital and perilous and hopeful as that of today's dreamers, who still set off across the desert seeking a better life in America more than a hundred years later."

—Alan Gratz, *New York Times* bestselling author of *Refugee*

"Alda P. Dobbs's stunning debut novel, set during the Mexican Revolution, recounts one girl's determination to save her family and follow her dreams. Inspired by the author's great-grandmother, *Barefoot Dreams of Petra Luna* is as breath-taking as a shooting star"

—Laura Resau, award-winning author of *Tree of Dreams* and *The Lightning Queen*

"A brilliant and authentic historical novel about a young woman's struggle for freedom. Petra Luna's dream will fill your heart with courage"

—Francisco X. Stork, award-winning author of *Illegal*

ALSO BY ALDA P. DOBBS

The Other Side of the River

BAREFOOT DREAMS
of Petra Luna

BAREFOOT DREAMS
of
Petra Luna

Alda P. Dobbs

sourcebooks
young readers

Published by Sourcebooks Young Readers, an imprint of Sourcebooks Kids
P.O. Box 4410, Naperville, Illinois 60567-4410
(630) 961-3900
sourcebookskids.com

Cataloging-in-Publication data for the hardcover edition is on file with the
Library of Congress.

Source of Production: Versa Press, East Peoria, Illinois, United States
Date of Production: June 2022
Run Number: 5025571

Printed and bound in the United States of America.
VP 10 9 8 7 6 5 4 3 2 1

TO MIKE, ANNABELLA, AND NATE.

THANK YOU FOR MAKING MY BAREFOOT DREAMS

COME TRUE.

AND TO ALL THE CHILDREN, PAST AND PRESENT,

WHO ENDURE THE HORRORS OF WAR.

THIS BOOK IS FOR YOU.

"No hay mal que dure cien años,
 ni cuerpo que lo aguante."

—Dicho Mexicano

"There's no curse that lasts a hundred years,
 nor a body that can endure it."

—Mexican Proverb

MAY 1910

A SMALL VILLAGE IN
NORTHERN MEXICO

CITLALIN POPOCA

The smoking star lit the night sky as women wept, holding their babies close. Men kept quiet while the old and the weak prayed for mercy. It was on that night that all of us huddled under the giant crucifix, the night when everyone—everyone but me—awaited the end of the world.

Everything was a sign to us *mestizos*, from eclipses to new moons to burned tamales in a pot. I learned early on that all signs were bad. When sparks flew out of a fire, it meant an unwelcome visitor would show up. A sneeze meant someone was talking bad about you. If a *metate*—a grinding stone—broke, it meant death to its owner or a family member.

But the biggest sign of all was *citlalin popoca*, the

smoking star. Papá's big boss at the mine called it a comet. It was some sort of a traveling star, he said, one that crossed our sky every so many years. To people like Papá's boss, that's all it was, but to us mestizos, it was the worst omen possible.

The Aztecs, our ancestors, saw smoking stars as an omen announcing the death of a king. We had no kings, only a man who had been president since before Papá was born, and had he died, I doubted anybody would have missed him. These days, a smoking star meant something different. It meant war and famine. Yet, others believed the star would come crashing down upon us, burning our homes and everything in sight. I didn't believe any of it.

There had been plenty of unwelcome visitors to our hut despite calm fires. Tiny babies sneezed all the time. Who could possibly talk bad about them? And I couldn't remember how many metates I'd broken in my life, but still, we were all kicking. My dream to go to school and learn to read had yet to come true. I did not plan on dying that night or anytime soon.

Little did I know that, soon enough, my world would turn into a nightmare. Still, in my heart, I believed that the smoking star wasn't to blame for halting my dreams or for taking loved ones away, or for bringing a war to my doorstep—a war so horrific and frightening, it reminded me of stories about the conquest of our people. Except this time our enemy didn't come from a faraway land. Our enemy lived among us.

SEPTEMBER 1913

one

LA PROMESA

There it stood, the perfect mesquite tree—thick branches, unburned, and without bullet holes.

I removed my shawl and lifted my long skirt high enough to climb. The tree's bark dug into my bare legs, but the pain from my empty stomach pushed me to climb higher.

"Petra, what happened to the pants you had?" asked Amelia, my little sister. She was six years old, half my age, and had a question for everything.

"Abuelita took them away," I said, steadying a foot on a gnarl. "She gave them back to Pablo."

My cousin Pablo and I were about the same height, except I was two years younger and twice as hardheaded, according to Abuelita.

"But they were your pants," said Amelia, putting her hands on her hips as she sat cross-legged. "Pablo gave them to you."

"I know, but..." I grabbed the branch above me and struggled to pull myself up. "Abuelita said girls have no business wearing pants."

In most families, girls had no business doing anything except learning to cook, clean, sew, and care for babies. But Papá was different; he always pushed us to learn more. At least he had until the revolution snatched him away.

"Mamá would've let you wear them," said Amelia.

I stopped at the mention of Mamá and turned to Amelia. She wore the dress Mamá had sewn for her days before she passed. It was brown with little yellow flowers. Amelia's only clothes were two dresses, and she wore this one almost every day. It was so soiled that it looked like winter had set on the little yellow flowers. And when I did the wash, no matter how much I scoured the dress against the creek's boulders, I could never bring spring back into it.

I turned back to the tree and pulled myself over the next branch.

"I miss Mamá," said Amelia, hugging herself and stroking her small, scrawny arms.

Half of my mouth gave Amelia a smile as I rubbed the sting and redness out of my hands.

"Do *you* miss her?" said Amelia.

I didn't answer. I couldn't. My heart was still too raw. Instead, I balanced myself to a standing position and grabbed another branch.

Mamá had passed a few hours after our baby brother, Luisito, was born, almost eleven months to the day. It still hurt too much to speak about her.

"Petra, be careful!" Amelia's dark eyes grew wide and nervous as I jumped from branch to branch, holding my small ax tight. This was her first time coming with me. She had convinced Abuelita to let her, claiming she needed to learn what I did. In reality, I think Amelia needed time off from looking after Luisito—probably her toughest chore.

I climbed up the tree as high as I could, found a comfortable spot, and began swinging my ax. It didn't take long to chop off enough wood to take into the village. Almost everyone in the village used coal, but after the mine Papá had worked in shut down, wood became the next best thing. Chopping and selling it was something I had to learn fast after Papá was gone, to keep us one step ahead of starvation.

Amelia helped me load our donkey with the wood, and I helped her mount it. She immediately wrapped her small arms around the animal's neck.

"I love you," she said to the donkey. "You're so hardworking and always smiling."

"He's a donkey, Amelia. Donkeys can't smile."

"Panchito can."

"Panchito? You named the donkey?"

It was a strict rule: don't name the animals. Names create bonds, and bonds tend to break, especially during war.

"I know Abuelita won't like it, but someone as hardworking as Panchito deserves a name, right? Promise you won't tell her?"

Promise. The word churned inside my head day and night. Six months ago, I had made the biggest promise ever when Papá was given the choice to join the Federales or be placed in front of a firing squad. On that day I had run across town looking for Papá, and when I found him, I knew he had chosen not to join. Papá stood against a wall blindfolded, his hands tied behind his back. He faced a line of soldiers with rifles aimed at him. All I heard next were my bare feet running across the line of fire toward Papá and my screams, begging to be shot along with him. I held on to Papá as two soldiers came to pull me away. I kicked with all my strength, and over my screams I heard Papá shouting for them to let me go, but the soldiers didn't stop until Papá said he'd join their war. Before Papá was dragged away, I promised to take care of Amelia, Luisito, and our grandmother, Abuelita. He then swore to return.

After a deep sigh, I turned to Amelia. "I promise," I said, convincing myself that in a world full of darkness and uncertainty, there was always enough room for one more promise.

LAS ESPERANZAS

Amelia and I entered our village through the main street and headed straight for the chapel. The chapel's front yard—the only one in the whole village—had a tall post where I tied my donkey every morning. I placed some woodpiles on my back and secured them with my shawl, then gave Amelia two smaller piles to carry in straw bags. We began our deliveries, zigzagging our way down each dirt street.

Morning noises filled the air in our small village. Soft claps of women making corn tortillas came from adobe cottages. Little boys holding sticks ran down the streets, laughing as they chased off dogs, pigs, and chickens feeding from the ditches. The village appeared to be as quiet as always, but things were far from normal. When

I was small, festivals were the only events that got everyone talking. People became friendlier during festivals as scents of cinnamon and brown sugar lingered in every street. At night, after a long day of celebration, I'd hold Papá's and Mamá's hands and watch the sky explode into a burst of colors. It made me feel as if nothing could ever go wrong. Things were different now. Our quiet village no longer had the heart to celebrate anything, and the only talk these days was about the revolution.

It was late morning by now, and Amelia and I took a shortcut through the village square to deliver our last batch. As we walked, we spotted three ladies wearing white silk dresses and walking in our direction. Their fancy, feathered hats were a sure sign of their wealth.

"Look," Amelia pointed. "Those ladies always smell like roses."

Right before the ladies passed us, one of them glanced at Amelia and wrinkled her nose like she smelled something bad. She grabbed the side of her dress and tucked it in, as though afraid Amelia's arm would touch it. Maybe she was afraid her dress would turn dark and ragged like ours, but more than likely, she didn't like our dark skin and flat noses.

Amelia gently tugged at the end of one of her braids. "I've always wanted to touch those dresses. They look so soft."

I had never felt silk before and didn't care to. People with silk passed me all the time. They ignored me, and I ignored them. I always kept my eyes on better things, like posters, banners—anything with big, small, or squiggly letters. Maybe one day, if I looked hard enough, I'd be able to figure out what they said.

Our village had no schools, and about a year ago, a lady was sent to teach all the kids to read and write. The happiest day of my life was going to her first class, but five days later, the teacher left and never returned. The revolution was to blame. Still, my dream of learning to read lived on.

I knocked on a large carved door for our last delivery.

"This is a pretty door," said Amelia, running her hand through the grooves. "Our hut would look nice with a door like this."

I shook my head. "I'd rather get a tile floor before getting a big wooden door."

"What's wrong with our dirt floor?"

"Nothing, it's just—"

Amelia interrupted me. "What's that smell?"

"Flour tortillas," I said.

"Flour?"

We never ate flour tortillas at home. They were always corn. Flour was a luxury reserved for the well-to-do.

"Don Raúl lives here," I said. "He's a sweet man. Sometimes he gives me one to munch on."

The door swung open, and a fancy lady stood on the top step.

"What do you want?" the lady asked with folded arms. She glared at our dusty, bare feet.

I lowered my eyes but kept my chin up. "I'm here to deliver your wood, ma'am."

"Speak louder. I can't hear you," said the lady.

I stretched my arm out. "Here's your wood, ma'am,"

The lady jerked the wood from my hand and slammed the door shut. My blood boiled.

Amelia glanced at me. "Was she supposed to pay us?"

I nodded and knocked on the door again. No answer. After the third knock, the door swung open again.

"What?" the lady said.

"It's two *centavos* for the wood," I said.

The lady's hard laugh pierced my ears. "You're telling me I owe you money for these sticks?"

The lady shook her head and walked across the room, mumbling to herself. After pulling two coins out of a jar, she stomped toward us.

"Here's your money," she said and threw the coins in our direction.

The copper coins clinked loudly as they hit and bounced on the steps where we stood.

My face burned; my jaw tightened. I grabbed Amelia by the arm and stopped her from picking up the coins. "No, Amelia. The lady can keep her money. Let's go."

"Oh, now you don't want it?" The lady smirked, hands on her waist.

Don Raúl entered the room. "What is happening?"

The lady motioned her head toward us, "These two barefoot *indias* want money for this cheap wood." The lady then pointed at the coins. "And now, the older one thinks she's too good for our money."

Don Raúl blushed and picked up the coins. "I'm so sorry, *m'ija*, here. Please, take the money."

"No, *señor*," I said. "Thank you, but I won't be delivering wood to you anymore."

"Raúl," shouted the woman. "Have you lost your mind? They're a couple of good-for-nothing orphans. Look at them. They're nobodies."

Don Raúl stepped outside and shut the door behind him, leaving the angry lady inside. He took a deep breath.

I fought back tears and pulled on Amelia's hand. "Let's go."

"*Muchachas*, girls, please," said Don Raúl. "I beg you, my wife gets a little frantic sometimes, but please, take the money. I know you need it. We all need it, especially with everything going on. Please, I'll feel terrible if you don't."

Amelia squeezed my hand. Her eyes begged me to take it because two centavos meant a good dinner— eggs, beans, chili, tortillas, coffee, and goat milk for her and Luisito. No money meant having to trade our chicken's eggs for milk to feed Luisito and growling stomachs for the rest of us.

I thought for a moment. "All right, Don Raúl. We'll take it."

Amelia didn't think twice and put out her hand.

Don Raúl dropped the two coins onto her palm.

"And here's an extra one," he said, pulling a coin from his pocket. "This is for helping out your big sister. It's extra, *de pilón*."

Amelia's eyes brightened. "*Gracias*, señor."

I helped my sister mount the donkey, and we began making our way out of the village up the main street. The lady's words still burned inside me.

"Why did the lady call us *indias*? Aren't we mestizas?" asked Amelia.

"We are, but people like her think poor, dark-skinned girls like us are indias."

"She also called us orphans."

"Probably because Mamá's gone," I said. Luisito's upcoming first birthday would mark one year since Mamá's passing.

"I thought *orphan* was when both your mamá and papá were gone. But Papá's coming back, right?"

"Of course he is. He promised," I said. Papá was a man of his word. He would come back. He had to.

Suddenly, a woman stepped out of her cottage and ran to the middle of the street.

"Julian! Julian!" She shouted her boy's name at the top of her lungs, over and over again. Her voice rang with fear. Another woman farther up the street came out and did the same, then another, and another. Before long, the streets echoed with the screaming and crying of women and children as everyone scrambled to get home. Then the men, with long machetes at their sides, ran for cover, shutting all windows and doors behind them as if expecting monsters to come.

Panic swirled around us, and fear rose inside my chest.

"What's happening?" asked Amelia.

I took a deep breath to keep my words steady. "I don't know," I said and wished Amelia had stayed back home. "We'd better get going."

A pair of shutters opened from a balcony, and a woman stuck her head out, the blood drained from her face. "Run, muchachas," the woman yelled at us. "Run and hide. The Federales are on their way. Run!"

I looked behind me down the empty main street. I could see a cloud of dust forming—the Federales about to storm into our lives.

I felt my heart drop into my stomach. Quickly, I pressed my lips together into a thin, hard line to keep them from quivering and to help me think straight.

My head swung to the opposite end of the road, to the small hill where our hut stood. The moment I laid eyes on our home, my insides twisted. Pablo, my cousin, would be visiting today. I didn't want to imagine all the horrible things the Federales would do if they found him. The hill seemed farther from us than ever before. Pablo's life was in danger if we didn't make it home in time.

I yanked on our donkey's rope with all my might.

"Hold tight, Amelia," I commanded. "The monsters are back."

three
LOS FEDERALES

Frightened and out of breath, I trudged uphill. My trembling hands grew damp, and it became harder to grip the donkey's rope.

Amelia crouched over her cherished animal, almost hugging him. She turned her head back to the town below us. Her scrunched up body quivered with every gunshot, and my feet scurried with every scream. The Federales were getting closer.

The Federales were the army of the government, of our current president, Victoriano Huerta, whom Papá had called a tyrant. This was the second time they'd charged into our village. The first time, they'd shot men as old as sixty and boys as young as eight for not joining them. They'd dragged Papá away and had also shot one

woman who'd protested against her sons' forced conscription. They were monsters.

Lately people had claimed that the Federales' desperate need for more recruits had turned them into
salvajes—people with no mercy or sympathy for life.
This frightened me and I dreaded the worst, not only
for Pablo but also for my family.

The enemy of the Federales were the *Revolucionarios*.
They were the rebels, the army of the people, who fought
to give peasants land and liberty. Rebels were like myth-
ical creatures. I'd never seen one, but I'd heard plenty
whispered about them: How they dressed, their bravery, and the women who fought among them. They hid
in the mountains, I was told, and ventured out only at
night. Unlike the Revolucionarios, the Federales never
hid and came out in broad daylight.

I helped Amelia dismount the donkey, then grabbed
her by the shoulders. I locked eyes with her. "If you see
Pablo, tell him the Federales are coming, to hide in the
hole."

Amelia rushed inside the hut through the front
door, and I ran around to the back to place our donkey
in the corral. I looked over my shoulder every moment,

hoping for enough time to help Pablo hide. A thought crossed my mind: What if the Federales were inside the hut already? I should have stopped Amelia.

With ax in hand, I rushed through the hut's back door. Our hut had no windows. It was a long, one-room adobe cottage divided by two large curtains, making three rooms. The first room I stepped into was Papá's. It was empty except for his bed, a frame standing on short legs made of thin poles held together by rawhide. His neatly folded sarape sat on top of his bed, waiting for his return.

The hut was quiet except for the bubbling sounds of the beans cooking. Abuelita's humming, Amelia's singing, and Luisito's cooing were missing.

I yanked the first curtain back and entered the second room. It too was empty. Amelia and Abuelita's bed was flush against the wall, and Luisito's tiny hay cot lay next to it. Papá's tool crate was on the opposite wall under Abuelita's shrine to the *Virgen de Guadalupe*, whom she prayed to and lit a candle daily to plead for Papá's safety.

I drew the last curtain. Amelia was startled as she clung tight to Abuelita's waist. Abuelita, despite her small size and the stoop old age had given her, stood proudly with her chin up. She rubbed Amelia's back and carried my baby brother, Luisito, close to her. Her tired, cloudy eyes showed no fear, unlike Luisito's, which were round like plates.

Next to Abuelita was a large wicker basket sitting on top of a straw mat. Both were used to cover a hole Papá had dug for hiding, a hole he never got to use.

Quickly, I placed my ax inside my waistband, then wrapped my shawl around my middle to secure the tool. I grabbed the *tranca* and dropped it into the notched stubs to secure the door.

"M'ija, that tranca isn't going to stop the Federales," said Abuelita.

I didn't answer. I ran to check on Pablo, but before I could reach the large basket, two shots rang out.

I held my breath.

We all stared at each other in silence as the clopping of horseshoes grew louder and louder until it reached the front door of our hut. The Federales were outside.

After three kicks, the tranca cracked in two, and an old federal soldier stormed in, yelling, ignoring both Amelia's screams and Luisito's cries.

"*Dónde está?*" he demanded. I could feel my insides contracting in fear; it was Pablo he was asking about.

"If you're searching for men, you're wasting your time," said Abuelita. "It's only us here."

"Everyone says that, old woman. You'd be surprised how many men hide like rats."

The soldier kicked at our belongings. He knocked over a pot full of beans and then kicked our coffee, Luisito's milk, and our warm tortillas into the fire. I ground my teeth as I watched two days' worth of work burn away. My thoughts went back to my cousin, Pablo. He was a brave boy who had never thought twice before protecting us, but sometimes he let his courage get ahead of his sense. I prayed he wouldn't do it this time.

A second soldier, a younger one wearing the same khaki uniform, came into the hut and joined the destruction. He used the butt of his rifle to break our pots, our crates, our *comal*, and our metate. I clenched my hands and tightened them every time Amelia screamed.

The large wicker basket was knocked over, and my breathing stopped. The soldiers, however, didn't notice the old mat in their frenzy. Abuelita and I exchanged glances. In her eyes I saw the same tension that burned inside me. If the Federales found the hole, even if no one was hiding in it, we would all be dead.

Surrounded by cries and clatter, Abuelita took a deep breath before speaking. "Gentleman, is this really necessary? You're not going to find any men inside those pots or crates."

The old soldier turned to Abuelita and slapped her, knocking her, Amelia, and Luisito to the floor.

Quickly, I huddled over Abuelita, giving my back to the old soldier, hoping my body was big enough to shield my entire family. The terror Luisito felt as he lay on the floor was expressed by sharp, piercing screams that further enraged the old solider.

"A boy was seen coming to your hut today," yelled the old soldier with his eyes bulging. "Either you tell me where he is, or you'll have to deal with us."

Abuelita said nothing. She winced and tried to soothe Luisito while Amelia cried uncontrollably and hid her face in Abuelita's side.

The old soldier took a step closer and squatted behind me. His voice, almost a whisper, was loud enough to be heard over Luisito's screams. "Perhaps you can tell me."

I shut my eyes tight and stretched my arms wider around my family.

"Hiding someone from us is a trespass punishable by death," he said. His strong breath of *pulque* made the skin on the back of my neck crawl with disgust. "Your abuela here is too old to know what's best. But you..." The soldier inched closer to me. "You seem smart, and I can tell you care a whole lot about your family."

He was right about the last part. Protecting Amelia and Luisito had been my main concern since Mamá's passing. The thought of anyone causing them pain angered me to no end, and it was that anger that kept me from talking. Besides, I knew better. I knew the Federales were not to be trusted.

"*Sargento*," said the young soldier. "What do you want us to take?"

The old soldier looked around. "Take that tool crate, the oil lamps, and anything else of value." As he stood up, he noticed something. "Arturo," he called the young soldier.

"Sí, mi sargento?"

"Look," the old soldier pointed to my bed. "I bet you someone is hiding up there."

Above the log beams that held the large curtains up

was my bed. It was a frame made of thin saplings fastened together with rawhide scraps. I used a notched pole that stood against the wall to climb up to it. I liked it up there. It was a good place for eavesdropping, always half-dark, and at times it kept me hidden from Abuelita or unwanted visitors.

The young soldier climbed up the notched pole. "*No hay nadie*, mi sargento. There's nobody." He climbed back down with my sarape and my black rock.

The old soldier walked toward him and grabbed my rock. He inspected it, bounced it in his hand, and then threw it over his shoulder.

My heart lurched, and my eyes followed the black rock as it fell into a puddle of spilled beans. I struggled to keep myself from rushing to grab it.

"Let's go," continued the old soldier. "We have to reach the next village before sunset."

The young soldier, with his rifle strapped to his shoulder, struggled to carry our belongings out the door. Fortunately, my hatchet was still with me. The other soldier, meanwhile, looked around our hut as if making sure nothing was left behind. He walked out without ever laying eyes on us again.

Different voices could be heard outside, but soon they were replaced by sounds of horses trotting over the rocky trail, fading into the distance.

Luisito's tiny chest fluttered with small, short sighs as Abuelita calmed him. Amelia sat next to them on the floor, wiping her eyes.

Slowly, I stood up and skulked toward the mangled front door, afraid any loud noise or sudden movement would bring the Federales back.

I ducked and peered out the door.

The trail was clear. The soldiers were gone.

I ran toward the hidden hole.

"Petra," said Abuelita. "There's no one in there."

I swung my head around. "Did Pablo not come today?"

"He did, but he left right away. He came to tell me he was joining the rebels."

"Joining the Revolucionarios?" My heart leaped at the thought of Pablo leaving the hacienda, but soon my excitement was overshadowed by anguish. What if Pablo couldn't find the rebels? What if the Federales found him first?

"Why would he do that?" I asked.

Abuelita's voice cracked. "He's tired of hiding, tired of the revolution, tired of waiting for your papá." She broke down sobbing.

Pablo's life had never been easy, even before the revolution. He grew up in a nearby hacienda, a large plantation, and was forced to work reaping wheat since he was six years old. The foreman always whipped his feet to make him work faster. Every cent he earned went directly to pay his papá's debt to the hacienda's store. It was a debt that had been passed down from his grandfather and would eventually be passed down to Pablo. Everyone knew that the debt could never be paid off no matter how hard you worked. And the rich plantation owners, the *hacendados*, knew this was the way to keep workers tied to their lands forever. It was slavery, only with a different name.

Suddenly, loud voices came from the corral. My stomach tightened. Had the Federales returned? I darted across the room toward the back door to listen better.

It all went silent and, as I cracked open the door, a soldier pushed it open and rushed in. He was a young boy, no older than fifteen. His face was red, and his hazel eyes were dazed.

"You have to leave," he said.

"Leave?" I asked.

"I have orders to kill you and your family and then burn down this hut." He leaned out the door, looked both ways, then turned back to me. "I'm going to walk out, go around to the front, and start the fire from there. Get out through this back door when I give you the signal."

"But...but where..." I scrambled to get my thoughts together.

"Listen. You don't have time," said the boy soldier. "Grab whatever you can, and get ready to flee through *el monte*. Use only the dirt trails, not the main graveled ones, because if el Sargento sees you, he'll make sure you and I both die."

"I need to grab our donkey, our chickens..."

"There's no donkey, no chickens," the boy continued. "The Federales took everything. Now, wait for my signal. I'll be at the end of the corral."

The boy ran outside, and I rushed to Abuelita.

"We have to leave," I said, helping everyone off the floor.

"I heard, but where to, m'ija?" asked Abuelita.

"I don't know," I said, looking at all the broken pots and crates, the spilled food and the burned tortillas. There was nothing to take. The Federales had taken what little we had left.

"What about Papá?" cried Amelia. "What if he comes back and we're not here?"

My eyes darted across our hut and over our shattered wares. Could we dig more holes? Find other ways to hide? The smell of smoke halted my thoughts.

"We have to go," I said. "We'll wait for him somewhere else."

The growing smoke made us cough as we stood at the back door waiting for the boy's signal.

The young boy reached the end of the corral, looked around, and signaled for us to go to him.

As we walked down the corral, I looked back. The roof was in flames, and suddenly, I remembered the one thing that had not been broken.

"Petra, where are you going?" asked Amelia.

"Keep going," I said. "I'll catch up with you."

I rushed into the burning hut, dropped to my hands and knees, and crawled across the long room. The smoke burned my eyes, and the flood of tears blinded me, but

I pressed on. I felt my way around the floor, across the broken crates and pots, until my hand found it—my black rock. It was the only thing I had left from Papá. I clutched it in my fist and ran back out into the corral. The young boy was directing Abuelita. "Go north," he said. "Everyone's heading that way. And take these to survive the night." He handed us sarapes. "Find a train soon to take you north because the desert and the Federales show no mercy."

Abuelita noticed my watering eyes. "Are you all right, m'ija?"

I used the end of my shawl to wipe my face. "I'm better now," I said, squeezing my black rock tight.

Abuelita turned to the boy and cradled his face with her hands. She'd often done this to Pablo. "Gracias, m'ijo. *Dios te bendiga.*" *May God bless you.*

The boy smiled and nodded with his eyes welled up.

I pulled Amelia by the hand, and we all rushed into the dense shrubs. Luisito, now strapped to my back, fussed as I helped Amelia climb up the rocky hill. My heart thumped loud over the shots still ringing from the village. I looked behind me and realized Abuelita had stopped.

With a hand over her mouth, Abuelita gazed down to the foot of the hill. Black smoke rose from what used to be Esperanzas. Rooftops burned, and bodies littered the streets. Women and children wailed and clung to men being dragged away to firing squads. Glints of light flashed when commanders dropped their swords, ordering the executions. I was startled with every shot fired until my vision of the entire village darkened. It was as if a giant cloud of coal dust had swallowed it whole.

My home, my life—everything I knew was gone. There was nothing to come back to. I thought about Papá and prayed that one day we'd find each other.

four

EL DESIERTO

Almost two hours had passed since we'd fled our home, and already my throat burned with thirst. The sun blazed, and our feet scurried down narrow trails that snaked in and out of thorny brush. We climbed across small canyons full of sharp, jagged rocks, trying to add as much distance as we could between us and the Federales.

"Can we stop now?" said Amelia. She staggered behind me. "My feet hurt."

"Mine hurt too," I said, slowing my pace. Abuelita trailed behind us, her wobbly knees barely keeping up.

I stretched my gaze to beyond Abuelita. Everything was the same behind her and in every direction. The treeless land around us had only dusty weeds and thorny shrubs that grew knee-high. At a distance, between two small hills, I could see part of the main graveled road.

"The brush is too short here," I said. "If we stop, the Federales might spot us. Let's go over the hill first, then we'll rest."

Abuelita and Amelia continued to walk without much to say. Luisito, still strapped to my back, slept.

Beads of sweat trickled behind my ears and down my neck like tiny lizards scrambling for shade. And no matter how many times I wiped my forehead, it dripped nonstop.

I helped Amelia and Abuelita climb the last rocky steps to the summit. Behind us, Esperanzas was out of sight. Ahead of us stood another small hill waiting to be crossed. The thought of climbing it made the bottoms of my feet burn.

"I have to stop, m'ija." Abuelita squinted and lowered herself onto a boulder. A plant as tall as Amelia with long, sword-shaped leaves gave the boulder a bit of shade.

Abuelita rubbed at her knees vigorously over the fabric of her long skirt. Amelia crouched between the boulder and the plant, trying to grab as much of the shade as possible.

"No hay nada," said Abuelita as she looked up and around. "Not a single bird."

Amelia peeked from under the thorny plant and into the sky. "Why do you need a bird right now?"

"Birds follow water," said Abuelita. "Especially in the mornings and in the evenings. They like to circle around it."

I looked around too. There was no chirping, even from the few trees down by the glen. Only the soft wind whistled through.

Papá had once told me that it took no more than three days without water for a strong, healthy man to die in the desert. I glanced at my family and wondered how we'd make it. Worry crept inside me, and I quickly took to one of Papá's phrases—keep busy, keep moving, and you'll keep worry at bay.

"I'll search for water while you all rest here," I said.

"No," Abuelita said, still rubbing her knees. "We need to stay together. Besides"—she glanced around once more—"I doubt there's water near us. Start looking for *sotol* instead."

A friend of Papá used sotol to make an alcoholic drink and *curanderas* used it for healing. I wondered if Abuelita wanted it for her aching joints.

Amelia pointed to the plant next to them. "Here's a sotol."

"No, that's *lechuguilla*," said Abuelita. "It's poisonous, unless you cook it for a long time. See how sharp the leaves are? They're like daggers." Abuelita turned to me. "Find some sotol, and use your hatchet to cut out its heart, but don't crack it open until you bring it to me."

Abuelita also asked me to gather *verdolagas*, *quelites*, *nopales*, and mesquites. When I unstrapped Luisito and handed him to her, he opened his eyes for a moment, then shut them back. His hair was drenched, and his cheeks were as red as prickly pears. Abuelita rested him belly-down over her lap and used the end of her shawl to fan some air over him.

"Go help your sister," said Abuelita.

Amelia shook her head. "I'm tired, and my head hurts."

"It hurts because you need water. Go with Petra. Start looking for sotol."

"I don't know what it looks like," said Amelia, still crouched beside the rock.

Amelia had gotten in the habit of saying she had a headache when she was sad or nervous. She'd done this since Mamá's passing. Her days full of chores—of watching Luisito, of helping Abuelita cook and clean— gave her no time for play, much less time to meet other girls her age. But Amelia acted as though she didn't mind and claimed our animals were her friends. Every free moment she got, she spent playing and conversing with our donkey, our chickens, or our goat. Amelia's headache now was probably because her beloved friends were gone; like Papá, they were with the Federales.

I brought my hand to my ear. "Amelia, I think I hear something down there."

Amelia straightened up and peered toward the glen. "What is it?"

"I think it's a dog or maybe a rabbit?" I said. "I can't tell, but I think it's calling out for you."

Amelia gave me a look like she was much too old to fall for that trick.

"*Ándele*, m'ija." Abuelita nudged Amelia with her elbow. "Go with Petra."

Amelia dragged herself up. White dust covered her bare feet up to her knees. Hand in hand, we followed the narrow goat trail down toward the glen.

"You see those mesquite trees?" I pointed. "I think that's sotol between them."

Amelia stopped and shaded her eyes. "I see some nopales too." She suddenly gasped. "And prickly pears." Amelia quickly let go of my hand and dashed ahead of me.

"Wait, Amelia," I shouted.

Right as she neared one of the trees, she halted.

Una cascabel. My stomach turned at the thought of Amelia coming across a rattler.

"What is it?" I asked upon reaching her.

Amelia stood motionless, staring at the ground. My eyes followed her gaze.

At her feet were three small heaps of stones, and planted atop each was a wooden cross.

"Are those people dead?" Amelia asked.

"I sure hope so. They're buried."

"How did they die?"

"I don't know," I said, guessing the desert had probably killed them. My eyes wandered up at the mesquite tree. On its lower branch hung three separate broken ropes. All three were tied to the trunk. I lost my breath, recalling a rumor about three young goat herders the Federales had hung for having run away from them.

I gave Amelia a gentle shove. "Keep walking."

Chills ran through my body despite the sun's relentless rays. With my hands trembling, I crouched in front of a large sotol near the three broken ropes. My head spun, and I didn't know if it was the heat or the thought of the Federales finding us.

"Is that sotol?" asked Amelia.

I took a gulp of air and nodded. After looking up to where Abuelita was, I scanned the landscape around us like a rooster sensing a hawk.

"What's wrong?" asked Amelia.

"Nothing." I wiped my face down and turned back to the plant. "You see how narrow and soft these leaves are, compared to the lechuguilla? See how these can bend?"

Amelia grabbed at one of the slender leaves. "But this one has thorns like the other one."

"It does, but these thorns aren't as mean-looking. Also"—I pointed to the base of one of the leaves—"see how it looks like a spoon down here? That's how you know it's sotol."

Amelia turned my way, trying to read me.

I forced a quick smile. "Go find some quelites while I figure out how to dig this root out."

Amelia smiled and walked away.

"Be careful," I called out. "Watch out for *alacranes* and *ciempiés*." Scorpions and centipedes were common this time of year.

Amelia stopped. "Is that what happened?"

I looked at her, puzzled.

Amelia motioned her chin to the wooden crosses. "Was it a scorpion or a rattlesnake that killed them?"

"*Quizás*," I said. "Perhaps. Or maybe something worse."

The sun hung low above the purple mountains, and Amelia and I helped Abuelita and Luisito come down the hill to rest under one of the mesquites. I spread out my tattered shawl on the ground and on it, Amelia and I laid our gatherings. Luisito, cooing and sitting over a sarape, clapped his hands and stretched out his arms to me, anxious to get the prickly pear I peeled for him.

I chopped up our third sotol and handed everyone a wedge. We all chewed on it and sucked out its fresh *aguamiel*. The juice tasted like raw cabbage with a hint of sugar.

Luisito, with a red-stained mouth from having eaten prickly pears, sat quietly, chewing on a piece of sotol. Suddenly he stopped, raised his head and wailed. Abuelita picked him up.

"What's wrong with him?" I asked, nervous his crying would become too loud for the quiet hills. "Is he still hungry?"

"No, I think he's teething," said Abuelita, bouncing Luisito on her lap. "Did you find the *candelilla*?"

"I did," I said, looking through our gatherings.

"Here," Amelia handed Abuelita a stem of candelilla with a proud smile across her face.

"*Muy bien*, Amelia," said Abuelita, scrapping off some the stem's wax with her fingernail. She pressed it between her fingers, then rubbed it against Luisito's gums. "This'll have to do for now, m'ijo."

Within moments, Luisito stopped fussing. He even smiled, wrinkling his nose and flashing his tiny, white teeth. Amelia and I looked at each other in awe.

"How do you know so much, Abuelita?" said Amelia.

"*Mi tata*," said Abuelita, before using her teeth to

tear off the end of a mesquite bean pod. Luisito probably had more teeth than Abuelita, but she claimed that the few she did have, even the broken ones, clung to her gums stronger than bark to a tree.

"It was my tata," said Abuelita, "who taught me about the desert."

I had always begged Abuelita for stories about her tata, her grandfather. Her face beamed every time she retold his old stories about Aztec gods or of his fighting for Mexico's independence. It was an independence he believed would change the mestizos' way of life.

Amelia stroked the fresh scrapes on her arms and legs. Unlike the long skirts Abuelita and I wore, Amelia's dress barely reached below her knees. Her exposed calves and shins had fallen victim to the sharp vegetation. The deeper cuts on her hands were from having helped dig out the sotol.

"Did Tata ever tell you why everything in the desert has thorns?" asked Amelia.

Abuelita chewed on mesquite beans and chuckled. Meanwhile, I reached for a small cactus paddle and broke it in half, then took the cool slime inside the plant and rubbed it over Amelia's scrapes.

"Gracias, Petra," said Amelia as she tried to hug me.

"Sit still," I said. "I'm trying to put some of this on your hands."

"I can't remember ever asking Tata about thorns," said Abuelita. "But if you ask me, I believe the desert is so harsh that every living thing in it has to grow thorns to protect itself. Some things, like the yucca and the lechuguilla, become bitter about the desert and grow poison within. Then you have things like scorpions and rattlers. Those resent the desert. They turn their bitterness into anger and spew their poison onto the innocent."

"I don't want to grow any thorns," said Amelia. "Thorns are ugly."

"M'ija"—Abuelita wiped the corners of her mouth with her fingers—"your first breath was in the desert. The cord that connected you to your mamá was buried under a mesquite tree so that you'd always be part of this land. You already have thorns, and thorns are beautiful—they make you strong." Abuelita spat out the chewed mesquite seeds. "Always be grateful for what you have. The day you take things for granted, your heart will swell with poison."

Amelia looked down at her elbow and rubbed it. "You're right, Abuelita. The other day I felt something prickly here, and I think—"

"Abuelita meant thorns in your heart, Amelia," I said.

Abuelita nodded. "*En tu corazón y en tu espírito.*" She patted her chest, pointing to her heart and spirit inside her.

With our bellies full of gifts from the desert, as Abuelita called them, we cleared the rocks off a small sandy patch near the mesquite trees, spread our sarapes, and settled in for the night.

Darkness soon gathered around us, and with it, the cool desert air and the distant howls of coyotes. Abuelita and Luisito slept and exhaled gentle snores. Amelia and I, lying side by side, counted stars as they appeared. Soon the sky looked as if it'd been sprinkled with diamond dust.

"Are you scared, Petra?" Amelia whispered.

"Scared of what?"

"Of the Federales or of never seeing Papá again."

"We'll see Papá again," I said. "And right now, I'm much too tired to worry about the Federales."

"How about *un apapácho?*" said Amelia. "Are you too tired for that?"

Unlike me at her age, Amelia never asked for a story or a song before going to sleep. Instead, she'd ask for an apapácho. If I had to guess, I'd say *apapácho* was Amelia's favorite word. It meant cuddling or embracing someone with your soul.

"Come here," I said and stretched my arms around her. I squeezed her tight and used one hand to pat her back. And like Mamá, I ended the apapácho with a head rub and a kiss on the forehead.

"*Te quiero mucho,*" said Amelia, declaring her love for me.

I responded just like Mamá would have, "*Y yo a ti te adoro.* Now go to sleep. We have a long day tomorrow."

Amelia snuggled closer to me and pressed her cheek against my arm. "You know what?" she said, facing the stars. "I'm not scared. As long as I'm with you, I know I'm safe."

Amelia's words weighed on me like a hundred bushels of corn, pressing heavy against my chest. I wanted to speak up and tell her that I was scared, that I had no idea how to keep us safe. Instead, I let her fall asleep without saying a word.

I lay restless for most of the night. My feet, my back, and everything in between throbbed. I wanted to stretch out the pain, but my muscles cramped with every attempt. My mind stirred too. I thought about my promise to Papá and how it'd been a constant struggle to keep in Esperanzas. I was now in the middle of the desert with a little girl and a baby in tow and an old woman with rickety knees. How would I ever fulfill it? And my dreams of learning to read and write—those drew further away each day. By now they were as distant and unreachable as the stars above.

five

EL AMPARO

The distant sound of a rooster's crow awoke me, but my tired eyes remained shut. I stirred under the sarape. My legs ached but my heart felt light, and as the fog inside my head cleared, I wondered about the day before. Had the Federales burned my home and my village, or had it all been a nightmare? I yawned and stretched my arms out, expecting to feel the wall of my hut, but instead they pushed against a thorny bush. I shot up and stared at the desert around me under the pink-purple sky, and when my gaze landed on the three broken ropes, my heart plunged. I was living the nightmare.

I heard the rooster's crow once more and remained still, trying to figure out its direction. A rooster meant chickens, eggs, and maybe a farm where we could find help. By the third time, I knew it came from the other side of the hill. I wiggled myself out from under the sarape.

Amelia opened her eyes and sat up. "Where are you going?"

"If Abuelita wakes up," I whispered, "tell her I went up the hill."

Amelia looked around, as if trying to figure out where we were, and as I turned to walk away, she grabbed at my skirt. "You're coming back, right?"

"I heard a rooster, and I think it's coming from the other side of the hill. I'll find out and be right back."

Amelia gave me a sleepy smile and sank back under the sarapes.

I climbed up the rocky hill as quietly as possible, stepping only on boulders and white, sandy patches. Halfway up the hill, I heard gentle sounds of twigs and dry grass being crushed. Quickly, I hid behind a cactus and peeked between the gaps of the thorny paddles.

Despite the silence around me, I remained hidden. My heart pounded as I pictured tall, black uniform boots stepping over the grass. The noise returned, and I forced myself to take a peek. To my relief, I caught a glimpse of a small coyote.

I stepped out from behind the cactus with my heart still pumping hard. "I thought you were someone else," I said with a sigh.

The scrawny animal took a small step from behind a yucca plant. His ears were pinned all the way back, and his sad eyes darted between the ground and me.

"Were you hiding too?"

A hawk screeched above us and, instinctively, the coyote shrunk back behind the plant.

"It's all right," I said. "It's only a hawk."

Slowly, the coyote came to its feet and stepped out with a limp. A large, dark stain covered his hip and hind leg. In the middle of it, a hole oozed with blood.

"You're hurt," I said, getting closer, thinking of ways to comfort him and wishing Amelia were here with me. She'd know exactly what to say or do.

My movements startled the coyote, and despite his injury, he jumped and limped away as fast as he could. From a safe distance, he turned to me one last time and disappeared into the dense brush.

Amelia swore that animals could smile, laugh, and even cry. I never believed her, but then again, I'd never seen an animal carry so much fear and sorrow, so much that I could see it eating him alive and harming him more than the wound itself. Perhaps Amelia had been right all along.

I reached the top of the hill. In the valley below was a burst of green next to a small stream. Tall *ahuehuetes*—sabino trees—fringed the banks as patches of green grass spanned from the river to a large building with a white cross sitting on top. A large bell hung from an arch above the entrance, and a cloud of smoke flowed from a chimney top. It was an old, stone church, and it appeared pink under the early light. A fence, made of stones piled high, surrounded it along with a small barn and a few cottages. Outside the fence, near the river, were rows and rows of towering corn stalks. Before long, I heard cows bellowing and goats clamoring to be milked.

I ran back as fast as I could to share the good news.

Everyone was up. Abuelita and Amelia folded the sarapes. Luisito, gnawing on a mesquite pod, took notice of me.

"Eh-ta. Eh-ta," shouted Luisito, pointing in my direction.

Amelia chuckled. "Sí, Luisito. It's Petra. Can you say, 'Amelia'?"

"Eh-ta," Luisito said again, holding his arms up to me.

"I found a church," I said, catching my breath and picking up Luisito. "They have chickens, goats, corn— I'm sure they'll help us."

Abuelita's face beamed. "*Vamos.*"

We rounded the hill instead of climbing it to give Abulita's knees a rest. When we reached the leveled land, Amelia rushed ahead.

"This looks like an old colonial church," said Abuelita. "Maybe an old convent."

Amelia reached the church and cracked open one of its giant, wooden doors. After peeking inside, she signaled us to follow her in. She was about to step in when Abuelita called out, "Amelia!"

Amelia squinted toward us, and Abuelita crossed herself repeatedly, urging my sister to do the same.

Amelia nodded and crossed herself a few times before disappearing into the church.

"It's a shame I haven't taken you girls to Mass more often," said Abuelita. "I'm afraid Amelia hasn't a clue of how to act in church."

I thought back to the last time we'd attended Mass.

It'd been at least five months, maybe six. Between my busy workdays and Abuelita's bad knees, attending Mass had become less frequent.

I switched Luisito to my left arm, and with my right hand, I drew my shawl over my head and followed Abuelita into the church.

I dipped my fingers in the small well filled with holy water and crossed myself. Luisito quickly grabbed my hand and inspected it, probably wondering why it was wet. Suddenly, I stopped and tipped my head back, taking in the high ceiling. The chapel was bigger than the one in Esperanzas but showed signs of disarray.

"What happened to all the pews?" I whispered to Abuelita.

She hushed me.

I continued to walk behind her and observed the niches on the walls. Some were empty or littered with broken pieces of clay. But despite the empty niches and lack of pews, people prayed. Dressed in tattered clothes like ours, they knelt across the bare floor with eyes shut. Their soft murmurs and the clicking of rosary beads filled the dark and damp air.

The smooth stone floor felt cool against my feet,

and above, sun rays slipped through small stained glass windows.

"*Mira*," I whispered to Luisito, pointing at the small rainbows formed on the whitewashed wall.

Amelia had reached the altar. She ran her hand over the marble slab where a large crucifix stood. Abuelita froze upon seeing this.

"*Ay*, Dios mío," Abuelita mumbled to herself and increased her pace toward Amelia.

"No, Amelia," said Abuelita, pulling her away from the altar. "Don't—"

"Can I help you?" whispered a young priest.

"Father," said Abuelita. She gave Amelia a stern look before turning back to the priest. "The Federales, *Padre*—they burned our home, destroyed our town... We have nothing."

"You've come to the right place," said the priest. "You'll be safe here."

Abuelita kissed the priest's hand. "Dios lo bendiga, Padre. God bless you."

Suddenly, the sweet smell of *pan pobre*, poor bread, hit my nose. The scent awakened my stomach and tugged strongly at my heart. I looked around, sniffing the air, wondering where the smell came from. It was a scent that had always brought feelings of comfort and safety. I didn't believe in signs, but if I did, I'd bet we were safe here.

six

PAN POBRE

Pan pobre was made out of corn. We called it *poor* because it was bread baked without expensive flour. But despite its name, pan pobre was still a luxury for us, and Mamá only cooked it during special occasions like birthdays or holidays. It was my favorite.

After his warm welcome, the priest led us to a dining hall. Over a hundred people, most of them dressed like us, lined the walls and waited for their piece of pan pobre. Our wait was short, and we each got a piece of bread, along with coffee for Abuelita and me, and goat milk for Amelia and Luisito.

My teeth sank into the steamy corn bread, and memories of Mamá and Papá flooded my mind. I let my eyes close, and as I chewed, I could hear Mamá's laughter from the last time she'd baked pan pobre for us. That day hadn't been a birthday or an anniversary. Instead, we celebrated a new beginning.

"I can't believe the revolution is over," Mamá had said joyfully. She fed Papá a small piece of warm bread with her fingers.

"Really, Mamá?" I asked as I prepared Mamá's favorite beverage—*champurrado*. Swiftly, I rolled the handle of the *molinillo* back in forth in my hands, frothing the milk as best as I could. "Is the revolution really over?"

"It is," said Papá. "And I've got proof." Papá reached for the coal-stained burlap sack he carried daily to work. From it, he pulled out a folded newspaper.

Mamá gave Papá a shocked look, but it was traced with a smile of understanding. Papá knew money was tight, and Mamá trusted there was a reason for his small splurge.

"I couldn't help myself," he said, looking at Mamá with the smirk of a kid who'd gotten away with eating too many sweets. "I had to buy it, because this here," he said, raising and waiving the folded newspaper, "this here is a piece of history."

Papá squatted and spread the newspaper over our dirt floor.

"Come look," he said.

Mamá, Amelia, Abuelita, and I gathered around him.

The paper's front page displayed a picture of Francisco Madero. I recognized him from the many newspapers I'd seen before on stands. Papá had long told me that despite Madero having been born into wealth, his heart had always been with the poor. Madero had opened schools for peasant children on his haciendas and paid all his workers well. Madero had also helped start the revolution that eventually overthrew Porfirio Díaz, a dictator who had ruled Mexico for more than thirty years. To Papá, and to many people I knew, Madero was a hero and a saint.

Sitting on my haunches next to Papá, I observed the photograph that took up almost half of the front page. In it, Madero wore a strikingly fancy suit and appeared to be inside a big room, reading to a group of men dressed like him. A single woman stood next to him, and under her beautiful hat was a face full of worry. My eyes fixed on her.

"My boss at work read this page to me," Papá continued. "It says that Madero is now our new elected president, that the revolution no longer exists, that it's dead. It also says that we have a new government that will work to make things better for everyone."

"Is that his wife?" I asked, pointing to the woman.

"It is," said Papá with a smile that would make you think he'd met them both.

"Why does she look scared?" I asked.

"Well," said Papá, pulling back. "She's probably worried about the road ahead, about the tremendous task of changing the way our country views itself and its people, even the poor ones like us."

Mamá took a deep breath. "I think she's worried for her husband."

We all turned to Mamá.

"Why should she be worried?" I said. "Her husband is the most powerful man in Mexico."

Mamá's concerned eyes steadied on the photograph. "I bet there are plenty of men in that room who covet Madero's power. She probably feels it."

Mamá's words had confused me that night. Had she meant that the other men were itching to be president after Madero? That they all admired him?

The celebration continued. We ate pan pobre and

toasted champurrado to our new president. Abuelita, Amelia, and I sang and clapped while Mamá and Papá danced the night away.

Later that night, before going to bed, Papá had let me see the newspaper once more.

"Soon, Petra," he'd said. "Soon you'll be able to read this piece of history yourself," Papá assured me as he proudly tucked the folded paper under his hay mattress.

Now, almost two years later, the revolution was back. Madero was dead, and that piece of history Papá had cherished so much was gone. It had burned down with our home, our lives, and our dreams.

It was early afternoon when the grown-ups gathered outside the church to discuss news of the revolution. The children were all sent inside to rest and nap in the chapel, away from the scorching sun.

Sitting on the chapel floor, I leaned my back against the whitewashed wall and watched Amelia and Luisito sleep on a spread-out sarape. We were steps away from the large, wooden doors, and from outside came the voices of men discussing who was to blame for the revolution.

"It's Porfirio Díaz's fault," said one angry voice. "For thirty years, he reelected himself president. He starved the poor and made the hacendados rich. He left us no choice but to start a revolution."

"No," said another man. "I blame Madero."

My ears perked up.

"I blame him," the man continued, "because after becoming president, he kept Díaz's old generals at his side. He should have gotten rid of them too. Instead he was naive and was later betrayed."

A feeble voice spoke up: "Who cares who's to blame? Our only hope now is that Villa, Carranza, and Zapata continue to lead the rebels and put an end to that traitor Huerta and his Federales."

"That's true," another voice sounded off. "Those Federales are brutal. Under Huerta, they're taking boys from orphanages and forcing them into uniform. They have to be stopped."

All the voices agreed and slowly faded away into the distance.

My throat tightened, and my heart squeezed as I

listened to the terrible things the Federales were doing and how people wanted them stopped at any cost. Papá, a good and honorable man, had been forced to be one of them. I wondered how many fathers, brothers, and sons had been forced to do the same.

I lay down and pulled out my black rock from the hem of my skirt. I brought it close to me. It was a piece of coal Papá had given me for my birthday two years ago. It was more than a black rock, though. It was a baby diamond.

"That's how diamonds are born," Papá had often explained. "When a piece of coal gets squeezed very hard for a very long time, it becomes a diamond."

He'd then squat and look into my eyes. "And you know something else, Petra? It's the same with people. When life's big problems squeeze you hard, you grow stronger. You grow up to shine like a diamond."

As my fingers traced the edges of the rock, I thought of Papá and wondered if I'd ever see him again. I brought my baby diamond up to my nose and smelled it. When I closed my eyes, I could almost see Papá coming home from work.

I was lost deep in thought when a girl's voice startled me.

"What's that rock for?" she asked. She looked younger than me and had blue eyes and a head full of brown curls that bounced over her shoulders. Her fair skin appeared as smooth as porcelain.

For a moment, I was speechless. The girl not only spoke perfect Spanish but her eyes, as blue as morning glories, looked at me like I was a dear friend. A girl dressed like her had never turned to look at me, much less spoken to me. I stared at her and wondered what she expected of me.

seven

EL INTERCAMBIO

I'd never been ashamed of my dark skin or full lips. Still, I often wondered what my life would've been like had I been born looking like the girl in front of me. Girls with fair skin were always spoken to better, they never had to wait in any line, and they always appeared cheerful and carefree. Girls with dark skin were expected to feel ashamed, to walk with their heads low and know their place in the world. Problems arose when you went against these expectations.

The girl lowered herself and sat cross-legged next to me.

"Hello?" she said and waved her hand across my face. "Can you hear me?"

"I can hear you," I said, still surprised she spoke Spanish. "You're speaking—"

"Spanish?" she nodded and then took a deep breath. "I was born in Mexico, so I'm really Mexican, but my mamá and papá are Americans. They live here. Well, my papá lived here until the revolution, and then he had to go back to Maryland. Do you know where Maryland is?"

I shook my head.

"Maryland is way, way up north. That's where we're going. But first we're meeting my papá in Texas, and then we'll go to Maryland. How about you?" She scooted closer to me. "Are you alone? Is that your baby there?"

"No. I'm here with my grandmother. He's my brother, and that's my sister."

"Are your mamá and papá coming to meet you here?"

I shook my head. "My mamá passed away last year after giving birth to my brother. My papá's fighting in the revolution."

"I'm sorry about your mamá," she said, pausing for a moment. "Is your papá fighting for *los buenos o los malos*?"

"I don't know," I said. The girl gave me a baffled look. Los buenos, the good people, and los malos, the bad ones, were different to everyone. Some loved the rebels for fighting for the poor. People who loved the Federales hated the rebels for having brought disruption into their lives. Early on, I'd learned to keep my mouth shut.

"My name is Adeline. What's yours?"

"Petra," I said.

"My mamá says Spanish names always mean something. What does yours mean?"

"It means rock," I said.

"Like the one you're holding?"

I looked down at my black rock and put it back in its safe place.

"My name doesn't mean anything," said Adeline. "But my last name, Wilson, is the same as the American president's. His name is Woodrow Wilson, but my papá says we're not related."

"Why didn't you leave with your papá?"

"My papá worked at a silver mine," said Adeline. "He was an engineer there, and when the bad guys came to his work, he had to leave fast before anyone saw him. Later, a man came to our house and gave us a letter from Papá telling us to leave and meet him in Texas. We took a coach and got here two days ago."

"Do you have brothers and sisters?" I asked.

"No." Adeline frowned. "It's just me."

Adeline continued to talk, and she talked a lot, but she also listened to everything I said. She shared her dreams of being an animal doctor, and I told her mine of learning to read and write. She told me stories she'd read about an orphan girl who lived with two evil sisters and another about a princess who'd been poisoned with an apple. I shared stories about Huitzilopochtli, the hummingbird of the south, who guided our ancestors through the wilderness to build Tenochtitlan, and about my favorite, Tlaloc, the supreme god of rain.

As the day turned to dusk, Adeline parted to go have dinner with her mother. Afterward she came to where I was sitting with my family and said she had something to show me.

Adeline led me to a corner in the dining area lit by candlelight. On the floor was a soft, scrunched-up blanket. Adeline sat next to it with her back against the wall. She patted the space next to her. "Sit here."

After I sat, she lifted the soft blanket and pulled something from under it.

"Do you know what this is?" asked Adeline.

My heart almost burst with excitement when I saw

a slate. I was so lost for words that all I could do was nod.

Adeline handed me the slate before covering our legs with the ivory blanket. "My mamá told me that when good, hardworking people have dreams, it's always nice to help make them come true."

The slate had letters written on it already.

"What does this say?" I asked.

"That's your name."

I took a second look at the slate. The white, chalky letters looked strong and beautiful. I ran my finger over my very own name.

"First, we're going to learn to write your name," said Adeline. "This is how you hold the chalk. Here, you try it."

Adeline wrapped my finger around the white, blocky stick. My hand trembled as Adeline guided me to outline P-E-T-R-A across the slate. I sounded out each letter along with her as I traced it over and over. I struggled to hold the chalk straight at first, but by my fiftieth time, I was able to write my name all on my own, without tracing it.

"So?" Adeline asked as I erased my name. "What happens now?" Her tone was sad.

"I write my name all over again and keep practicing," I said, steadying the chalk over the slate, pretending to have misunderstood Adeline. I was sure she meant what would happen after the church, but I didn't want to think about it. Not right now. I wanted to keep chatting, to keep learning. I wanted to, for a moment, forget all my pain and anguish. My day with Adeline had been like a sweet *siesta*, and I refused to be awoken.

"No, I mean where will you go from here?" she said. "You said the boy soldier who helped you escape told you to go north, but where north are you going?"

My lungs filled with air, and the fine chalk dust lingering around us made my nose twitch. I brought the pencil down and glanced at my name halfway written. It looked broken.

"I don't know," I said. "Maybe we'll stay here until we can go back to Esperanzas."

"But your village is gone, right? You said it was burned down."

I cast my eyes down. "It was, but that's where my papá will return."

"Tomorrow, my mamá and I are going all the way into America, across that big river that joins the two countries."

"El Río Bravo?" I asked.

Adeline nodded. "My mamá told me people are safe once they cross that river."

I imagined a river as wide as the sea, one wide enough to keep bullets and cannon balls from flying across.

"I was little when I went to America," said Adeline. "I don't remember much, but my mamá says there's a school down the street from our new home, and I'll be going there as early as next week."

The thought of going to school in America made my heart skip. I knew America lay north of us, but I had no idea how far it was, much less how to get there.

Adeline brought out a tiny bundle wrapped inside a white cloth. Gently, she pulled back the folded corners, and to my surprise, in the middle of the cloth was a piece of pan pobre.

"I saved this from dinner," said Adeline. "I like it so much, I wanted to eat it and share it with you while we talked."

I smiled and grabbed the half Adeline offered.

Adeline didn't talk much as she ate her piece, but her eyes fluttered with each of the four bites it took to eat it.

"You like this bread?" I asked.

Adeline nodded repeatedly as she licked the crumbs off her fingers. "I've never had bread like this before."

"I know how to make it," I said.

Adeline gasped. "You do? Can you teach me?"

My chest swelled knowing I could return a favor. I dictated the ingredients and instructions for pan pobre, and Adeline wrote them on her slate. She assured me her mamá was good at memorizing recipes.

"Do you know how to make that thick *atole?*" asked Adeline. "The one that has cinnamon and chocolate in it?"

"Champurrado?"

"Yes," said Adeline, bouncing up. "My mamá loves that stuff. Our neighbor made champurrado all the time but never wanted to share the recipe with us. Can you believe that? She'd always say, 'I'm sorry. It's a family recipe. It's a family secret.'" Adeline tilted her head side to side as she mocked her neighbor.

"And you know what upset me the most?" By now, Adeline's ivory face had turned as red as a chili pepper. "Every time our neighbor refused to give us the recipe, she'd slurp her champurrado and remind us how good it was." Adeline blew a puff of air in frustration and rolled her eyes. "My mamá finally gave up asking."

I chuckled at Adeline's funny faces. "Well, you're in luck because my mamá used to say I made the best champurrado in northern Mexico." I boasted.

After Adeline notated the champurrado recipe, she threw her arms around me. "Gracias, Petra."

I didn't tell Adeline, but recipes were also family secrets for us, and if Abuelita knew I'd just given *two* away, she'd probably have a *patatús*. I understood all about not sharing recipes, but after a long day with Adeline, she felt like a sister to me.

Suddenly, a tall, blond woman with striking blue eyes approached us.

"Petra," said Adeline, standing up, "this is my mamá."

I shot up and stood straight.

Adeline's mamá smiled and brushed my hair back with her long, slender fingers. She said something in English, and I quickly turned to Adeline to learn what she'd said.

"My mamá says you're a pretty girl," said Adeline.

I lowered my eyes as warmness flushed through me. My dark skin and almond eyes had offended people many times. It was nice to be seen differently.

Night fell, and after Adeline and I exchanged good-nights, she went back to her mamá and I to my family.

As I lay between Abuelita and Amelia, I told them about how I had learned to write my name. With my index finger, I traced invisible letters in the air. *P-E-T-R-A*.

In the half-lit room, I saw Amelia's eyes widen. "Maybe you can be a teacher one day."

Abuelita chuckled. "Being a teacher takes more. You have to go to school, buy books—it's for people who live in a different world than ours."

"I can go to school and learn to read in my world too," I said.

"You're trying to change who you are, and that'll drive you crazy," said Abuelita. "Accept things as they are. Besides, knowing to write your name is a lot more than your mamá, your papá, or I ever knew."

"I want to learn to write my name too," said Amelia. "Can your friend teach me?"

Abuelita pushed air through her nose. "Barefoot dreams," she muttered and turned to her side, facing away from us.

"I'll ask Adeline tomorrow," I said to Amelia. "I'm sure she'll say yes."

I turned back to Abuelita. She had always scorned my talk of letters, teachers, or learning to read. Her words had never bothered me, but now that Mamá and Papá were gone, they stung.

"Why did you say 'barefoot dreams'?" I asked.

Abuelita remained silent and still.

Amelia and I exchanged glances before she gently patted Abuelita's back. "Abuelita, Petra wants to—"

Abuelita gave an exasperated sigh and turned to us.

"Wanting to learn to read is a big dream, and big dreams are dangerous," said Abuelita. "You'll do better when you accept things as they are, when you accept your lot in life."

I closed my eyes for a moment. Those words—*lot in life*—always turned my insides; they made me feel sick.

"Petra, I know you mean well," said Abuelita. Her tone had softened. "But dreams like yours are barefoot dreams. They're like us barefoot peasants and indios—they're not meant to go far. Be content with what you have."

I thought back to my village, to Esperanzas. No one there knew how to read or write, except for the well-to-do. That bothered me, but what angered me the most were people like Abuelita who simply accepted it.

I'd had a good day, and I wasn't going to let Abuelita's words ruin it. I lay down, shut my eyes, and steered my thoughts to Papá. He saw things differently and even urged us to be different. Thinking of him made me smile, and I counted my blessings for the day. I had a new friend, a stomach full of pan pobre, and a hopeful heart. And to top it all off, I had learned to write my name. Perhaps, despite the revolution or my bare feet, the stars above weren't all too distant.

eight
EL ESCAPE

Early the next morning, Adeline woke me up with a gentle shake. "Want to eat pan pobre with me?"

I followed Adeline to a long room where breakfast had been served the day before. We each grabbed a piece of corn bread, a cup of goat milk, and sat side by side on a bench.

Adeline was quiet, and I wondered if she was still sleepy.

"Thank you for teaching me to write my name yesterday," I said.

Adeline nodded with a serious face, dipping her corn bread into the milk.

"Are you all right?" I asked.

"Do you think we're safe here?"

I glanced around the room. It was filled with families and groups of kids sitting on the bare floor or on benches flush against the wall. They were eating, talking, laughing—nothing appeared out of the ordinary.

"The priest said we were safe here," I said. "Why do you ask?"

"My mamá looks worried. I haven't seen her this scared since—" Adeline stopped and shoved the last big piece of corn bread into her mouth.

"Since when?"

Adeline chewed without answering, looking away.

I turned back to the people in the room. I observed their faces, especially the grown-ups. None seemed to show any worry. I looked around for the priest but didn't see him.

Adeline gazed at the cup she held over her lap. "I think my mamá heard something bad, but she won't tell me."

"What do you think she heard?"

"I don't know; maybe something bad is about to happen." Adeline sniffed and wiped her nose with the back of her hand. Her eyes remained fixed on the cup.

"I'm scared," she whispered.

"Don't be," I said in the gentlest voice. "You're with your mom, and pretty soon you'll be with your—"

"It's you I'm scared for," Adeline said, turning to me. Her eyes and nose were red.

I forced a hopeful smile. "We'll be fine."

"Not if we all have to leave. Where will you go?"

I felt Adeline's nervousness starting to seep into me. I took a deep breath to stop it.

"Last night I thought about asking my grandmother what plans she had for us," I said, "but I think she was tired. She fell asleep fast."

Soon after having said this, I lowered my eyes. I felt bad not having been completely honest with Adeline. Abuelita's scolding about my barefoot dreams had stopped me from sharing the idea of going to America. Especially because it'd been something Adeline had suggested. I knew it would not have sat well with Abuelita.

Adeline sighed before turning back to her cup. "I used to have a sister."

I paused for a moment. "What happened to her?"

"She fell off a horse. She passed last year."

"I'm so sorry. Was she younger than you?"

Adeline shook her head. "She was four years older,

but we still played a lot together. She used to read me lots of books, and some nights we'd stay up late sharing all kinds of stories." Adeline turned to me. "Talking to you yesterday reminded me a lot of her. I really miss her."

I nodded. "I know how you feel. I always miss my mamá."

"My sister lived for two days after the fall, and my mamá paced around her as she lay dying. I'd never seen my mamá so scared before. But last night, after she talked to the priest, she had that same frightened look."

"What did he tell her?"

Adeline shook her head repeatedly. "I don't know." She then set the cup down beside her and turned to me. "Let's make a deal."

"A deal?"

"Yes, how about we—" Adeline stopped when a man rushed past us and climbed onto the bench beside us.

It was the priest. His face was red and full of anguish. "Attention everyone," he shouted. "Attention."

All eyes were on the priest, and suddenly, he seemed at a loss for words. The priest's hands, held together as if in prayer, pressed against his lips. He slowly scanned the faces around him.

Quiet tension filled the room. We all stared at him, wide-eyed, anxious to hear his words.

"The Federales," the priest managed to say. "They're on their way."

Screams erupted across the room.

"But this is the Lord's house!" cried a lady.

The priest nodded repeatedly. "It is the Lord's house, but this revolution is turning men into monsters. A priest was killed yesterday, and his church was burned down."

Adeline and I glanced at each other.

"I urge you all to leave now," the priest continued. "There's a train station east, about two days away."

People stood up and quickly gathered their children and what little belongings they had.

Adeline turned to her mamá, who stood at the door and spoke to two men wearing tailored suits. She looked concerned, and as she talked, she signaled for Adeline to go to her. Adeline glanced at me with spooked eyes before running to her mamá.

Words were exchanged between Adeline, her mamá, and the men. Adeline shook her head a lot while pointing at me. Within a moment, she was back.

"Petra." Adeline's breathing was shallow. "My papá sent those men to take us north."

"Can they take us too?" I asked without hesitation.

Adeline frowned. "I asked, but they said there's only room for one more person in the automobile they brought. Come with us, Petra. Please."

I felt a pinch inside my chest as I looked back at Abuelita. She spoke to other people while Amelia, beside her, rocked Luisito.

"I can't, Adeline. I'm sorry."

"But if you come with us, I'll teach you to read. We'll go to school together and we'll talk all night long and—"

"Adeline." I grabbed her hands. "I can't leave my family here. I made a promise."

Adeline stretched her neck to glance at Abuelita. "Your grandmother looks strong. She can take care of Amelia and Luisito. And once the revolution is over, you can come back."

I wanted stability in my life. I wanted to go to school. But my dream was meaningless if I didn't stick to my promise.

"I'm sorry, Adeline," I said. "They need me."

Adeline threw her arms around me and cried.

I squeezed her back. "We're going to be fine. I made a promise to my papá, and I mean to keep it."

Adeline pulled back and took a quick glance at her mother, who motioned urgently for Adeline to join them. She turned back to me and, through tears, gave me the same friendly smile she'd given me when we met the day before. My heart felt heavy, and I didn't know if it was because of the unknown that lay ahead or from seeing Adeline so heartbroken.

"Take care," said Adeline. She gave me a quick embrace before running back to her mamá, and for the last time, she glanced at me before walking out.

I pushed myself through the anxious crowd, toward Abuelita.

We packed our sarapes and added food and water to our load. With Luisito strapped to my back, I tightened my shawl and pushed open the church doors. The blinding light hit me, and the hairs on my skin rose when the warm morning air brushed against them.

Everyone marched east, away from the lush surroundings of the church and into the white dust of the desert. Fathers and mothers who shared the load of small children and belongings walked quickly ahead of us. The ones holding the lead were the families in wagons that left big clouds of dust behind.

I turned behind me. Abuelita waddled, holding Amelia's hand. Amelia faced back at the church, and when she turned to the front, tears streamed down her cheeks.

"Amelia." I evened my pace with hers. "We're going to be fine."

Amelia nodded with her lips curled down, wiping away tears.

I had to be brave for Amelia, but I was scared. I didn't know what lay ahead, and the thought of leaving Mexico, of going to a new country, frightened me, because if we left, we might never see Papá again. More than ever, I needed his love and his guidance. I needed someone to show me how to survive, someone to hold me and tell me everything would be fine.

Luisito's tiny hand reached from behind and touched my face. It was a warm touch like the ones Mamá used to give me when she knew I was scared. His hand, soft on my face, provided strength but also reminded me how much I'd promised to protect. I grabbed Luisito's hand, spread his tiny fingers open, and kissed the center of his palm. I prayed with all my heart that everything would turn out well and that Abuelita knew where to lead us.

nine

EL TIGRE SUELTO

It didn't take long for people who had escaped with us to shrink in the distance. By now, they had all turned to puffs of dust before vanishing into the horizon. These were the people who'd been friendly and courteous to us at the church; some had gone as far as to share food with us and even nurse Luisito. But once out of the church, no one had stopped to help us. Instead, they turned their gaze away. They saw Abuelita as too old, my siblings too young, and all of us too weak to outrun the Federales. Not to mention we'd be extra mouths to feed.

As the sun moved higher in the sky, I reminded myself to shorten my strides so as not to leave Abuelita and Amelia behind. With every step, the ground grew hotter and the jagged rocks poked deeper under my feet. The desert's intense glare was blinding, but despite it, I felt as if we were walking in darkness, as if we'd been thrown into a void where questions about Papá, our lives, and our future echoed in the emptiness and went unanswered. I hated this uncertainty, especially with no one to guide me.

Twice I had tried asking Abuelita where we were going, and twice she had silenced me. She had instructed us not to speak much. Talking made you thirsty, she'd said, but I didn't think it worked. I'd been quiet almost all day, and still, my mouth and throat felt as if I'd swallowed a whole sac of *pinole* without a drop of water.

We crossed a dry arroyo before coming across a small, quiet hill. The sun, just above the mountains, shot warm, orange rays across the purple sky. Abuelita suggested we stop for the night and ordered Amelia and me to spread out our sarapes.

As we all sat facing each other, Abuelita split our last piece of corn bread into four pieces. She handed me the largest one. "Here, m'ija."

I began to nibble on my piece slowly in case Amelia asked for more.

"Abuelita," I said. "What happens tomorrow?"

Abuelita fed Luisito without acknowledging my question, and Amelia's eyes, tired yet wide, turned to me and then to Abuelita.

I swallowed. I didn't know if Abuelita hadn't heard me or if she'd purposely ignored my question. I tried again, a little louder this time. "Abuelita, do you know where we're going tomorrow?"

When Abuelita's eyes turned to me, I knew she'd heard me both times.

She took her time to answer, as if thinking of what to say.

"I reckon we keep walking," said Abuelita. "We'll keep walking until we come across another church or a hacienda where we can get help."

"But the priest didn't mention another church or hacienda nearby," I said. "He only said there was a train station—"

"Two days away," said Amelia.

"That's right," I said. "And if we've already walked a whole day, we'll probably reach it tomorrow."

Luisito stuck his tongue out and blew air out of his mouth. He made noises and spat out pieces of corn bread Abuelita had fed him.

"Are you done, m'ijo?" Abuelita asked. She tried feeding him again, but Luisito turned his head and pushed her hand away.

"What about after we reach the train station?" I asked.

Abuelita took a deep breath. "I don't know. Maybe we stay there, if there's a town."

"What if the Federales attack it? What then?"

"Ay, m'ija, I don't know," said Abuelita, throwing her hands in the air. "I really don't know. What do you want me to say? I guess we'll just have to keep running."

"Keep running until when?" I asked. "When do we stop?"

Abuelita's shoulders dropped as she put a hand over her eyes.

I scooted closer to her, and my hand reached for her shoulder. "How about we go to America?"

"Do you have any idea know how far it is?" said Abuelita. "What makes you think we'll reach it by foot?"

"We can find the train station first," I said, "and then take the train north to America. I heard it's safe there."

"But even if we get across," said Abuelita, "it's a whole new country. We don't know anyone there. We don't even speak the language."

"What about Papá?" cried Amelia. "He'll never find us if we leave Mexico."

"Amelia's right," said Abuelita. "Even if we don't know where we're going or what's going to happen, it's best we stay put. Otherwise your father is never going to find us."

My stomach—twisted with Abuelita's indecisiveness—no longer felt hungry. I put my piece of corn bread down and stepped away.

The sun was gone, and a few scattered stars had begun their early glow. In the dusk, I could still see the mountain's purple ridges. They looked as strong as the ridges of my baby diamond that pressed hard inside my palm. I closed my eyes and let the warm mountain breeze carry me to a cool February evening earlier that year.

That night, I had joined Papá outside amid the darkness, and as a frigid chill swept down the mountains, I raised my shawl over my shoulders.

After Mamá's passing, Papá's evening ritual involved gazing at the dark, starry sky to gather his thoughts. I often joined him to do the same or to simply share my grief in silence.

That night was different, though. Papá stared at a

distant storm coming over the mountains. The tempest pushed a blanket of dread across the desert that seemed to smother the last bit of calm in Papá.

"What's wrong, Papá?" I asked timidly.

Papá stopped a sigh from escaping his lips and swallowed it. "President Madero was killed this morning." His voice was as solemn as if he'd lost another family member, and my heart crumpled, not for the president but for Papá's anguish.

"How?" I asked, sure it'd been an accident because the revolution had ended a little over a year ago.

Papá lowered his gaze to the ground. "Both Madero and his vice president were executed this morning."

The word *executed* dropped heavily on me, like an ax on a log. It hadn't been an accident. Someone who didn't like Madero or his ideas had killed him. A person like that frightened me.

It took a while before I could speak again. "What happens now?"

Papá turned back to the storm. "I don't know."

I shivered at Papá's words. He'd always had an answer for everything, but in the darkness, Papá's silhouette looked tired, defeated.

The next day, our village cried and mourned Madero's death. People said the revolution, the one that had gotten rid of a dictator, was about to return. Only this time, it would strike Mexico like an angry tiger that had just been unleashed.

"The revolution missed Esperanzas the first time," an old man had said, "but this time, blood will run down every street in Mexico."

He'd been right. It now seemed as if blood ran down every street, even down the most hidden desert trail.

Papá's uncertainty in February had frightened me as much as Abuelita's hesitation did now. Uncertainty seemed to always invite havoc and strife into our lives. But I knew. I knew there was a safe place. I also knew there was a train a day's walk away that could take us there. I knew exactly what we had to do.

"We're going to America," I said, speaking from my gut.

"Eh-tah," said Luisito, pointing at me. He then blew air and bubbles through his mouth.

"What about Papá?" asked Amelia.

I was about to respond to Amelia when Abuelita interrupted. "I've told you already, we don't know a soul there."

"Abuelita, all the people we knew were in Esperanzas," I said, "and Esperanzas is gone. It's been destroyed. We can't go back there, not for a long time."

I turned to Amelia. "And if we stay, the desert or the Federales will kill us before Papá has a chance to find us."

Abuelita remained silent, considering my words. Under the moonlight, she had undone her braids and now ran her bony fingers through her thin, white hair. She let out a heavy sigh. "People at the church said that starvation is everywhere to the south. I was even told that in some places, the living look like walking skeletons. Maybe the famine is coming this way."

"It's already here," I said, picking up the piece of corn bread I'd put down.

Abuelita filled her lungs with air and began to braid her hair. "Maybe you're right. Maybe we should head north and see what happens before crossing to America."

"You think Papá will look for us even if we go to America?" asked Amelia.

"Papá will go to the ends of the world to find us," I said. "I know he will."

That night I lay down exhausted but relieved. I had

a sense of direction, and it was enough to bring me a sliver of hope. I couldn't wait to rise in the morning and start our march. Tomorrow, we'd see the same sunset and the same beautiful purple sky, except this time, we'd be riding aboard a train that would take us all the way into America.

ten

EL EQUILIBRIO

Two days had passed, and still there was neither sight of tracks nor the sound of a distant train whistle. The rolling plains had flattened and were full of sandy patches and dead brush. We were out of food and water, and the desert appeared to have been stripped of all its gifts. Every cactus patch we saw was a mere stump. Sotol plants lay dead with missing hearts. And not a single shred of quelites or verdolagas could be found. It'd all been scavenged away.

Poisonous yucca and lechuguilla abounded. Some, as tall as oxen, provided shade and relief from the blazing sun. But if you weren't careful and got too close, their sharp leaves would rip through your flesh like a soldier's sword.

Disheartened, I continued to lead my family, recalling the frightened coyote and refusing to let fear eat at my soul.

The sun, almost halfway across the sky, burned hotter than the day before. It was white-hot, and its rays pierced through our skin like tiny cactus needles. Nothing stirred in the intense heat except for the wind lifting the scorched earth.

"*Otro remolino*," said Abuelita. She pointed to a dust devil forming ahead. The spinning dirt charged toward us, and Abuelita lifted her shawl over her head. Amelia turned away and tucked her face under her folded arms. I quickly ran to put myself between Amelia and the swirl. I took Luisito off my back and braced him against my chest, under my shawl. I squeezed my mouth and eyes shut.

The wall of dust pushed through and lifted my hair. Tiny grains of sand slapped hard against my face and blew into my ears and nose. The one good thing about a dust devil was that it didn't last long.

I fluttered my eyes open. The dust clung to my eyelashes like soot on a chimney. I puffed air out of my nose to clear it. Despite having had my mouth shut, bits of desert rolled across the top of my tongue and down my throat.

I pulled Luisito away from my chest. He'd slept through it all. Amelia coughed and rubbed her eyes.

I patted her back. "Are you all right?"

Amelia gave a tired nod. Her drooping eyes were as red and swollen as her blistered feet.

Papá had once said that walking barefoot toughened you, and he was right. Running over stones had never bothered us. If we stepped on a sharp thorn, we'd simply brush the *espina* and sting away against the dirt and continue to run. But we'd never had blisters like these before, blisters that made the tiniest thorn feel like a flaming knife.

I strapped Luisito to my back again as we continued our somber march. We followed a narrow, sandy path—an old miner's trail—that'd been used to transport coal before the train. I'd found it the day before and was sure it'd lead us to the train station.

My thoughts went to Adeline, wondering if she'd made it to el Río Bravo by now, or maybe even to Maryland. I tried to imagine Adeline arriving at her home in America and her joyful reunion with her father. I imagined her introducing me to him and then him welcoming me into their family. I imagined myself in new clothes, going to school, and spending long nights with Adeline, reading books and sharing stories. These visions put a smile on my face, and though at times my feet questioned my decision of not having left with Adeline, my heart knew I'd made the right choice. I'd have new clothes someday, and I'd go to school as soon as we reached America. But not seeing my brother and sister through this wilderness would have tormented me my entire life.

I kept my head low to avoid the bright light that scorched my eyes every time I looked at the horizon. Besides, there was nothing good to see. The same barren land surrounded us as far as the eye could see, and the small wooden crosses, like the ones we'd seen under the mesquite, seemed to have multiplied the deeper we got into the desert. They'd become so common that Amelia no longer questioned how the person had perished.

I took a quick glance at the horizon and made out something in the far distance. My hands rushed to shade my eyes. It was a thin, white line that stuck up from the ground. It looked blurry as it wavered in the smoldering heat.

"Look," I said, turning back. "There's a—" My heart seized. "Where's Amelia?"

Abuelita looked behind her. My eyes frantically scanned the trail, its surroundings. There was no trace of her. It was as if the desert had swallowed her whole.

As Abuelita yelled out Amelia's name, I tightened my shawl to secure Luisito and sprinted up the trail, retracing our path.

My heart thrashed inside my chest. I wanted to shout Amelia's name, yet my dry throat locked, not from heat or exhaustion but out of fear. It was a fear that slithered up my spine and wrapped itself around my neck, not letting me breathe.

I ran as fast as I could and didn't stop until my chest burned with fire, until my lungs felt like they would explode. Slowly, I caught my breath and brought my trembling hands up and over my eyes to scour the landscape.

And there, under a yucca plant about a hundred steps away, was Amelia. She stood motionless with her head hunched.

My throat opened. "Amelia," I shouted and raced to her.

Amelia looked up but didn't answer. Her eyes were sunken, and the color on her face was gone. Blood and dirt caked over her cracked lips.

"Amelia, what's wrong?" I squatted and grabbed her shoulders.

Amelia looked down at her feet. "I can't walk."

I glanced down. Amelia's feet were covered in blood.

"Can you carry me?" she asked in a soft voice.

I'd carried Luisito for two days, and my back felt as if it were about to break.

"I've got Luisito on my back already," I said. "Can you try walking a little more?"

Amelia reached for my hand. Her straw-thin legs shook as she tottered. She suddenly caught sight of the vultures above, and her legs gave out.

I gripped Amelia by her armpits, but we both dropped to our knees.

"The *zopilotes*," she cried. "They're going to eat me."

"No, they're not," I said, looking up at the ugly birds. "They're only sniffing for food."

I rubbed Amelia's head. My knees had begun to stiffen, and I struggled to rise to my feet. "Come. Stand up."

Amelia's lips quivered. "I can't."

I looked around at the desert's emptiness and exhaled a big puff of air.

"Petra," Abuelita hollered from a distance. She wobbled toward us. "*Qué tiene Amelia?*"

"She can't walk," I shouted back.

Amelia sobbed. "I didn't want to stop, I promise, but my feet hurt too much."

A few tears streamed down her face. Each drew a clean, fine line over the grime.

"It's all right," I said. "Don't cry. You're wasting water." I used my shawl to wipe her face. "Abuelita will take Luisito, and I'll carry you."

I handed Luisito to Abuelita and helped Amelia climb up my back. Amelia's weak arms wrapped around my neck. I reached back for her legs and shifted my hips to adjust my back to her weight. Still, it felt like it would split in two down my spine. Amelia was three times heavier than Luisito, and with each staggering step I took, blood and pus seeped from the bottoms of my feet.

"Hold on tight," I said. My head swayed with dizziness.

Amelia squeezed my neck and gently kissed the back of my head. "I love you."

Despite my aches, I couldn't help but tease Amelia. "Do you love me as much as Panchito?"

Amelia gave a weak chuckle. "More."

We continued our trek, and the white line I'd seen before in the horizon became clearer. It appeared to be a tall cross or a sign of sorts. I was desperate to reach it, but spasms of pain shot through my legs as I strode. I shortened my steps to lessen both the pang and Abuelita's lagging.

My arms shook as I lowered Amelia to the ground. I stretched my neck and rubbed the cramps from my shoulders, taking the last steps to the white line.

The white line turned out to be an old, weathered signpost. It stood about a foot taller than me and had three white, arrow-shaped boards nailed to the top. Each board had words painted in black and pointed to a different direction. My entire body grew limp when I realized we'd reached a crossroads. The trail we'd been on was splitting into three separate paths.

"What is it, Petra?" asked Amelia.

I opened my mouth, but a knot in my throat snatched my words. I looked back to Abuelita. She was about fifty steps away.

"What does it say?" asked Amelia.

I didn't answer. My eyes went wild. They roved between each of the three trails and the boards above. I only recognized a few letters from my name, but the rest made no sense. Why hadn't I been smarter? Why hadn't I asked Adeline to teach me to write something more useful like *train* or *station*?

A heavy, invisible force pressed down on my shoulders. The force pushed through me, reaching my soul and sapping away my last shred of strength. I fell on my haunches and hung my head. I wanted to cry but had no tears. I wanted to scream but had no strength. Instead, I cracked open my mouth, and a small squeak escaped my lips. I'd been defeated. I would never fulfill my promise to Papá or shine like the diamond I longed to be. I'd remain a lump of coal for the rest of my life.

Suddenly, the wind picked up and blew hot as if someone had opened the door to a giant oven. Hot air rushed across the desert and then against me, spitting dirt at my face. A cough gripped my body as I choked with the dust. I doubled over in pain but more so in rage.

My coughing came to a stop, and with my next breath, I let out a howl.

I grabbed fistfuls of sand and hurled them at the sign. I screamed at it, cursed it, and separated flesh from fingernails as I dug into the earth. Unable to grasp enough sand, I crawled and picked up rocks, sticks—anything I could throw at the sign.

"Petra!" Abuelita grabbed my shoulder.

I yanked away and spotted a bigger rock near the base of the sign.

"M'ija, *por favor*." Abuelita grabbed my wrists as I lifted the rock. "*Mírame*," she said in a firm yet loving tone. "Look at my eyes."

Panting, I lowered the rock and tried to steer my wild eyes to hers.

Abuelita took the stone away and turned me around by the shoulders. "Lean on this." She tapped on the post.

I sat back with my chest still heaving. Abuelita squatted next to me and placed her hand over my heart. She closed her eyes and ordered me to do the same.

"Remember the *chicharras* back home?" she said.

Remembering bugs was the last thing I wanted to do.

"I told you to close your eyes," said Abuelita. "Shut them now."

I closed my eyes half-heartedly. The desert was silent,

but inside my head, a battle took place. Voices as loud as canons mocked me and accused me of being hopeless, of being simple, and demanded over and over that I quit. The voices boomed louder when I shut my eyes.

I filled my lungs with air and combed through the snarl of thoughts in my head. By my third slow breath, my mind was able to relive the cicadas from back home.

"Remember their song?" asked Abuelita. "At first, it's only one chicharra that buzzes." Abuelita inhaled before making a long shushing sound. "Then, a second one buzzes. *Shhhhh...*" Abuelita's shush had grown stronger. "Then another...*shhhhhh*...and another...*shhhhhh*... Before long, hundreds of chicharras sing together."

Abuelita's gentle shush mimicked not only the cicada's song but also the sound of leaves ruffled by an autumn breeze.

"Match your breathing to their song," said Abuelita. Between breaths, Abuelita's shush started out gentle and then grew louder before trailing off into stillness. She repeated this over and over like ocean waves Papá had once described to me.

"Come back to nature," said Abuelita. "Connect yourself again."

Abuelita's hand, still pressed against my heart, poured warmth into me. As my lungs swelled and dropped to the rhythm of her sound, the heaviness inside me lifted away.

I opened my eyes and met Abuelita's.

"Better now?" she asked.

I forced a smile.

"There are spiritual energies all around us," said Abuelita, "in the rocks, the earth, the wind—they're all willing to help, but if you're out of balance, they can't reach you."

Abuelita shifted from her knees to her haunches and sat on the ground next to me. "Who cares what the silly sign says. You only need nature to guide you." Abuelita released a deep breath as loose silver strands from her braids danced in the wind.

"Our ancestors' ashes, sacred and full of wisdom, lie across this land," said Abuelita. "And when the wind blows, it sings the knowledge of our ancestors to the desert." Abuelita turned to me. "Learn to keep your mind quiet so that you can listen to the singing of the wind."

If nature really guided us or if the wind really sang, I

asked myself, why hadn't it told me where the train station was? And if nature couldn't talk to me because I was out of balance, why didn't it talk to Abuelita instead?

"Remember those big *papálotl* we see flying every fall?" Abuelita asked.

The image of Amelia and me chasing after those big butterflies brought me peace. The bright orange and black wings, so elegant and silky, always left us spellbound. We never caught one. Never wanted to. All we wanted was to watch their graceful fluttering in the wind.

"Those butterflies have a very important job," said Abuelita. "They carry our ancestors' souls back home on the Day of the Dead. Do you think they need signs or fancy maps to tell them where to go? No, they look to nature to lead them."

I caught Amelia watching us in silence. Her mouth was cracked open like a bird's beak on a scorching summer day.

I glanced at the sign above. I was calm, but deep inside me lingered a tiny twinge of frustration. Abuelita must have sensed it, because she rubbed my back.

"Knowing to read and write is like riches, Petra," said

Abuelita. "You can't take them to the afterlife. But bravery and principles of truth and generosity, now, those are treasures that'll stay with you long after you're gone. They'll help guide your children, and your children's children, in any wilderness."

I sat up and looked behind me, at the three separate paths.

"How do I..." I cleared my throat of dust. It burned when I swallowed. "How do I find balance?"

"You find balance when you connect to nature and your past—your roots," said Abuelita.

"But how?" I asked.

"Open your eyes, your ears, and your heart to the world around you." Abuelita cradled my face in her hands and smiled. "Be still. With practice and patience, you'll learn to listen."

I sat in silence and observed the desert's great vastness. I was ready to listen.

Abuelita adjusted Luisito on her back, then turned to Amelia. "When curanderas are about to give a good *limpia*, they sent the person out into the desert first to prepare them."

I'd had a couple of limpias, spiritual cleansings,

when I was Amelia's age. In the ritual, my body had been swept with a raw egg to absorb all the negative energies.

Abuelita continued, "We must think of this journey as a preparation for the biggest cleansing of our lives."

Amelia's tired eyes lit up a bit. "Then we're going to need eggs this big." She stretched her arms out wide.

Abuelita chuckled. "You're right, m'ija."

Amelia crawled over and cuddled with me. "I'll help you listen too, Petra."

I smoothed Amelia's hair back and kissed the top of her head, tasting the desert in her hair.

I stood up and helped Abuelita to her feet. The air around us had grown hotter. It would be another scorching afternoon. My eyes scanned the landscape, and as the sun cooked my skin, my mind was ready. I was ready to listen to Mamá, to Tata, and to all of my ancestors. I was ready to observe nature and let her guide me. I was ready to fulfill my promise.

eleven

EL SOLDADO

Nature's first cue was a tall boulder, darker than the color of the earth that stood not far from us. I threw my shawl over the scalding rock and climbed it. Once on top, I eyeballed each trail.

All three paths disappeared into the line where the desert met the sky. Only a distant band of pale rocks stood out. It snaked almost parallel to the trail on the far right and appeared to be clear of brush. It was a creek bed, but it ran bone-dry.

"I can't tell where the trails lead to," I said to Abuelita.

Abuelita's face looked thoughtful and a bit concerned.

"I did see an arroyo." I pointed to the direction of the creek bed. "But it's dry."

Abuelita's eyes widened. "Let's go to it."

"To the arroyo?" I said. "Why not follow one of the trails instead?"

"Take me to it, m'ija. I'll show you," said Abuelita.

I shrugged my shoulders and led Abuelita to the ribbon of rocks. She had Luisito on her back, and I had Amelia on mine. Halfway to the creek bed, Abuelita glanced back.

"What is it?" I asked.

"There's a small tilt to the ground," she said. "That's a good sign."

We reached the band of rocks. It was the width of three men lying end to end. I put Amelia down and handed Abuelita one of the creek's pebbles, like she'd asked.

Abuelita took the pale stone and ran her thumb over the rounded edges. She brought it to her nose and cracked a smile. "Smell this." She handed me the rock.

I twitched my nose over it like a rabbit. "I can't smell anything."

"Are you sure?" said Abuelita.

I tried again but nothing.

"The rock's spoken to me," said Abuelita. "Let's follow this creek bed."

I let Abuelita walk past me and quickly brought the rock up to my ear. I heard nothing. I even shook it a little but no luck. I threw the rock away before Abuelita could turn to see me.

"Vamos," she said.

I took Amelia up on my back again.

"Did the rock tell you something?" Amelia whispered in my ear.

"It didn't," I said.

Many times I thought Abuelita told tales to give us hope or make us feel better.

"How about your rock?" said Amelia.

"My rock?"

"Your baby diamond. What does it tell you?"

I thought for a moment. "I don't know. I don't think I've ever put it to my ear."

Amelia and I didn't speak much afterward. My head throbbed with pain, and the tingling in my arms grew stronger. To keep my mind off my aches, I thought back to my baby diamond.

Come to think of it, my little black rock had told me a lot. Its rough edges—the ones that'd reminded me of Papá's hands and how hard he'd worked at the mine—told me he was working just as hard now to get back to us. The rock's dark, grainy surface told me of the storms Papá was facing in the desert as he fought to get back to us. And the rock's resourcefulness and strength, well, that was like Papá's heart: rich, solid, and enduring till the end.

We continued our trek down the creek bed. From time to time, we'd pause for a break and I'd grab a rock for Abuelita. She'd eyeball it, touch it, smell it, then hand it to me to mimic her inspection. All the rocks had felt the same to me, and none had smelled like anything.

After having smelled what seemed like a wagonload of creek pebbles, I finally got the tiny, subtle whiff of rain. I gasped.

"You smelled it, right?" Abuelita grinned. "The rock's finally spoken to you."

I smiled and held the rain-smelling rock under my nose. Next thing I knew, my hands loosened. I dropped the rock, making a loud clank. I stood frozen, awestruck.

I blinked a few times and realized that twenty steps away, down the dry bed, was a miracle. Nature's marvel. Water.

Trickles of fresh, pure water seeped straight from the rocks. The dribbles were small, but they gathered

like flowers in a bunch and formed a beautiful, boun-
tiful brook.

I took Amelia up in my arms and ran to the brook. I
sat her next to me, almost dropping her on the brook's
edge. We both plunged our faces into the water and
drank handfuls without stopping. I turned back to
Abuelita, who was beginning to unstrap Luisito.

I dipped my cupped hands into the water to take
some to Abuelita. I noticed that downstream, short
trees began to line the brook's fringes. The creek widened farther down and led into what appeared to be
a large water hole. My heart pounded when I saw the
outline of a village looming on the horizon beyond
the water hole. Earth-colored huts lined the edge
while the pink tower of its church stood at the center.

"Petra," Abuelita shouted. "Luisito—he's burning."

I ran to Abuelita and reached for Luisito's forehead.
His hot skin made my heart sink into my stomach. I
grabbed him and rushed to the water.

"*Mójale la mollera primero*," said Abuelita, keeping
behind me and urging me to moisten his head first.
"Mother of God, with everything that has happened to
us, it's probably *susto*."

Susto was a malady brought about by a terrifying experience. It made the soul want to flee the body. If the susto was small, a spoonful of honey or sugar brought the cure. If it was big, the suffering child had to have their head splashed first. The rest of the body was then dipped in water to shock the soul back.

"Or maybe it's *mal de ojo*," cried Abuelita, kneeling next to me. "Someone gave him the evil eye."

I splashed Luisito's head, then submerged his limp body underwater.

Abuelita reached for his shoulder when I pulled him out. "*Dios mío*. He's still on fire."

"There's a village over there." I nodded downstream. "I can look for a doctor."

"No," said Abuelita. "Find a curandera. He needs a limpia."

I shot Abuelita a stare. Luisito needed a doctor right now, not a spiritual healer. But there was no time to argue. I dipped my shawl in the water, soaked it, and then wrapped it around Luisito's naked body.

"Promise me you'll take him to a curandera first?" said Abuelita. "Promise me, Petra."

Amelia sobbed as she stared at us.

I agreed with hesitation.

I held Luisito's warm head against my chest and bolted. My bare feet lifted in the dust, not feeling the thorns or sharp rocks beneath me. I flew past the water hole, and within minutes, reached the village.

The town was similar to Esperanzas before it'd been burned down, but it had an appearance of mourning. The dirt streets appeared empty except for two women sitting on a sidewalk. Both had ragged, blue shawls wrapped around their heads.

"Excuse me," I said between breaths. "Where can I find a curandera?"

The ladies looked at each other. "We had two curanderas in this town," said one of the women, "but both left for the revolution."

"There's a pharmacy around the corner of *la plaza*," said the other woman. She pointed down the street toward the town square. "You might find a doctor there."

"Thank you," I said and ran off.

The pain in my back and the burning of my feet were gone. It was as if my legs had dissolved in the desert, and now the wind, having taken pity, carried me.

The pharmacy stood on a corner, and I rushed in

through its open door. A girl wearing a simple cotton blouse and dark, wool skirt stood behind the glass counter. She greeted me.

"My brother—" I said, "he needs a doctor. Is there one here?"

The girl nodded. She tiptoed and leaned over the counter to see Luisito. I took him off my chest and brought him up to her.

She touched his red, clammy face and snapped her hand back. "Virgen María." She crossed herself. "Wait here."

The girl raced to the far end of the counter and disappeared behind a door. I couldn't make out her words, but her voice was full of urgency. The other voice was coarse and dry.

I neared the cracked door. Through its gap, I observed a man with a long, white mustache and a stringy beard like that of a billy goat. He wore spectacles and sat on a chair, overlooking an open book on his desk.

"But I felt the baby, Doctor," said the girl. "It's a really a high fever."

"Ay, Rosa," said the man with his eyes on the book.

"You know how broke I'd be if I treated every person like her that came in here?"

"But Doctor—"

"You heard me," said the doctor, rubbing his beard down without looking up. "Ask her if she's got money. If she does, I'll see her. If not, ask her to leave. Simple as that."

There was a brief silence before the girl answered, "Yes, Doctor."

The girl returned with a face full of anguish. "Do you have any money?"

I nodded. On the counter I placed my hatchet and the coins I'd earned from my last wood deliveries. "This is all I have."

The girl pressed her lips and forced a smile. "I'll be back." She went behind the door again, leaving the coins and hatchet behind.

The doctor's voice grew loud. It echoed in the empty pharmacy. "Are you serious?" He blew air through his teeth. "That's barely enough for a few tortillas. Tell her to leave."

The girl was about to walk away when the doctor called her back.

"Rosa, make sure you clean the floor after she leaves. I can't stand the filth those people bring in."

I looked down behind me and saw the trail of bloody footprints over the polished floor.

The girl gathered my coins and handed them back to me along with the hatchet. "I'm so sorry. It's not enough, and the doctor wants you to leave."

As I stored my belongings away, I glanced at the shelves lining the pharmacy's high walls. There were as many bottles and tin cans as there were stars in the sky. One of those would probably make Luisito better.

"Do you know where I may find help?" I asked.

The girl sighed. "This place has been a ghost town for a while. Perhaps you can sit out and ask for money."

Her suggestion sparked anger in me. For generations, no one in our family had ever begged for alms, even in the worst of times. Papá had often said, "When life puts you in a hole, the only way out is through hard work." Begging was a slam to our name and our beliefs. It meant losing all honor and becoming *gente sin nombre*, nameless people.

"You mean beg for alms?" I said.

"No, not beg. I mean asking people for help."

"I've never begged for money," I said, standing as straight as my tired back allowed. "I won't start now."

The girl stooped her head and nodded gently.

Outside the pharmacy, I spotted a tall, round fountain in the middle of the square. Water didn't rain from its tall feature like it did in Esperanzas. Upon closer inspection, the fountain's basin held weeks' worth of dust and debris without a single drop of water.

I sat on the edge of the circular basin and brought Luisito down from my shoulder. He was as hot as before, but this time small shivers swept his tiny body. He needed help.

The entire plaza and the streets surrounding us were desolate. Even the trees appeared to have no birds. Suddenly, I caught sight of a small ray of hope above the trees—the church's pink tower.

"The church," I whispered to Luisito. "They'll help us there."

I cut through the plaza, ran across the street, and shot up the church's steps to the tall, wooden doors. As I reached for the iron handle, I noticed a chain wrapped around the handles of both doors. A padlock secured the cold metal links and hung still between the handles, like a pendant on a fancy woman's neck. I jerked the padlock a few times, shaking cobwebs and dust from it.

"The church's closed," said a woman's nervous voice. She stood below the steps.

"Why?" I asked.

The woman looked both ways and lowered her voice. "The priest was killed about a month ago, and all the nuns disappeared. It's been locked since."

All sorts of questions flocked into my head. I wanted to know who'd done such monstrous thing and why. I wanted to ask where to get help, where the train station was, but the woman scurried away like a frightened mouse.

I leaned my back against the church doors and cradled Luisito close to me. His skin was the color of ash, and his parched lips were slightly open. His body no longer shivered.

"Luisito." I shook him gently. "Wake up."

Luisito fought to open his eyes. He gave a small sigh before shutting them again. His flickering eyes reminded me of Mamá's on the morning she passed. She'd fought hard to keep her eyes open, to smile and to tell us everything would be fine. Those images, alive in my mind, and now Luisito's sweltering body were like blows to the gut.

Helplessness engulfed me and weakened my body, and as my knees bent, I slid down the church doors and hummed an old lullaby to bring Luisito and me some calm.

After Mamá's passing and Papá's forced departure, villagers had expected me to go to the streets and beg for alms. I never did. Instead, I picked up Papá's hatchet and taught myself to use it.

Now, I sat in a strange village, on the steps of an abandoned church, holding my sick brother. I didn't have enough money for a doctor or the energy to chop wood. All I had were my family, my name, my honor, and my dreams.

I pulled Luisito closer, shut my eyes, and then did something I swore I'd never do.

I bowed my head and stretched my arm out. And as I begged for alms, a blanket of shame fell over me. It felt heavy, suffocating. My eyes welled up in frustration, and anger took over my lullaby, turning it into a jumbled tune. I was angry at my helplessness, angry at my lack of power, and angry at the world for stripping layer upon layer of dignity off my soul.

People passed and murmured. Some voices revealed sorrow and asked God to bless me. In others I heard disgust, saying it was people like me who'd caused the revolution. My hand shuddered with every coin dropped in it, as if each was a burning coal of disgrace. I kept my head down, refusing to see the peeve and pity in people's eyes.

Not long after, I heard heavy steps. Each tread carried the sound of rattling spurs. I fluttered my eyes open and saw a pair of tall, black boots across from me. A deep voice came from above. "You're not crying, are you?"

I shook my head, wiping my eyes and nose. I looked up.

In front of me stood a woman. She wore dark leather pants, a white linen shirt, and a short, wool jacket. Her shoulder-length hair was pulled back. She had a pistol on each side of her hips, one cartridge belt around her waist, and two more that crossed her chest. What stood out most was the purple scarf around her neck. She was a *soldada*, a woman soldier.

"Is that your kid?" asked the soldier.

"No," I said. "He's my brother."

"What's wrong with him?"

"He has a fever, and it's getting worse. I took him

to the doctor down the street, but he wouldn't see him unless I had money."

The soldier wrinkled her brow, looking in the direction I'd pointed.

After a moment, she stretched out her hand to me. "Come. We have a doctor at the camp."

I leaned Luisito over my shoulder and grabbed her hand, and as she pulled me up, she said, "I'm Marietta, by the way. Marietta Torres. What's your name?"

"Petra," I said. "Petra Luna."

"Follow me, Petra. We'll take my mare."

I hesitated to walk.

"My grandmother and sister are outside the village, near the water hole." My voice trembled. Marietta looked like a tough soldier. I didn't want her to think I was asking for too much and take back her offer.

"They're not far from here," I said, "they're—"

"We'll send for them." Marietta gave me a half smile before walking again.

Swept with relief, I followed.

Marietta didn't wear the typical khaki uniform of the Federales, yet she was loaded with enough bullets to scare any federal soldier. She had to be one of the rebels;

she had to be a Revolucionaria. Perhaps she'd seen Papá, or maybe even fought against him. Regardless, I would keep my mouth shut and take whatever help I could get.

twelve
EL CAMPO MILITAR

I had never ridden a horse before. I'd ridden donkeys, mules, and even on an old steer Papá had owned when I was little, but never a horse. Only people of means or authority rode horses. Even though I rode sidesaddle without holding the reins, there was a sense of pride riding such a powerful animal. But maybe it wasn't the mare. Maybe it was Marietta and the way people acknowledged her as we trotted through the camp.

Right as we entered, half-dressed children with bright eyes ran alongside us, shouting, "*Capitana!*" They all scrambled for Marietta's attention. The women, grinding corn over their metates or scrubbing clothes in pools of water, raised their heads at the commotion and greeted Marietta with joy, "Buenas, mi capitana."

The men stopped what they were doing and greeted her; some even brought their hats down over their chests. Marietta never smiled, but she acknowledged everyone's greeting by tipping her head.

The entire camp was spread out like a giant picnic that stretched as far as the eye could see. People clustered themselves under mesquite trees or under colorful sarapes spread on poles. Some men cleaned their weapons while others slept or played cards. The women cooked and cleaned or tended to their babies.

Marietta dismounted and immediately ordered a man and a woman to fetch Abuelita and Amelia. Without hesitation, the two climbed on their horses and galloped off to the brook by the water hole.

I looked at Luisito and was relieved to feel his temperature coming down a bit. Perhaps the horse ride had helped.

"Follow me," said Marietta, pointing ahead of us.

Up a slope and behind hundreds of campers was a train. It was an enormous beast made of black iron. Trains had often stopped at the mine in Esperanzas to pick up coal, but I'd never seen one this close.

I increased my pace to keep up with Marietta. Her

long strides took me down a string of wagons lined back to back. After passing countless boxcars, Marietta swiftly climbed up the iron steps of one of them. It had a giant blue cross painted on its side. She extended her hand and helped me climb up.

I followed Marietta through a narrow door. The boxcar we entered had white, smooth walls and a single bed in the center.

"This is the operating room," said Marietta. She led me into another, similar car and then to one lined with three bunk beds on each side. "The sick ward," she said, turning her head back slightly as she walked.

We passed two more boxcars with beds, all empty of people, and then reached one that looked like a small pharmacy.

"There he is," said Marietta, approaching a man who stocked the shelves. "Good afternoon, Dr. Johnson."

"Captain, it's good to see you," said the doctor.

Marietta gave the doctor a strong, firm handshake. Almost immediately, I stopped listening to the words being spoken between the two. My attention was on how they spoke to each other, their posture— especially Marietta's. I was in awe. She stood tall with her shoulders thrown back and her chin held high. The doctor was a blond, blue-eyed man, and he spoke to Marietta, a dark-brown mestiza, as if she were a town's magistrate.

"Could you lay the baby here for me, please?" The doctor patted a small table.

"Sí, señor," I said.

The doctor pressed and tugged at Luisito's skin. He looked into his mouth and peeked into his loosely shut eyes. He began running his thumbs over the sides of Luisito's neck. "When was he last fed?"

I looked at Marietta and then back at the doctor. "He hasn't eaten today. Yesterday my grandmother tried to feed him chewed maguey leaves, but he'd spit them out and fuss."

The doctor placed a few drops into Luisito's mouth. "This should take care of the fever, but he needs to be fed soon, otherwise he won't have the strength to fight whatever infection he has."

Marietta glanced at me. "We have plenty of food here for you and your family."

The doctor handed me a small bottle with a dropper. "Give him two drops tonight and two more in the morning for the fever. If he gets worse during the night, come and get me."

"Thank you, doctor," I said and offered my coins to him.

The doctor pushed my hand back with a smile. "No need to pay me." His gaze dropped to my feet and then to the bloodstains behind me. His smile faded.

The blood rushed to my face. With Luisito over my shoulder, I dropped to my knees and took the end of my shawl to wipe off the mess I'd made.

"I'm so sorry," I said when the doctor's strong hand grabbed my arm. He lifted me as if I were a baby bird who'd fallen off its nest.

"Leave it," he said. "I'll clean it later. First, I'll need to look at your feet."

I turned to Marietta. Her lips stretched thin and revealed two deep dimples. She nodded once.

The doctor laid Luisito on the table, and then he and Marietta helped me on top.

"Your feet are a little torn," said the doctor. His eyes smiled at me. "Nothing we can't fix."

With bandaged feet, I followed Marietta out of the boxcar and walked with her through the camp. We headed toward a dusty *huizache* tree where I could see Amelia and Abuelita.

"Petra!" said Amelia, trying to talk through a mouthful. "Look!" She smiled and triumphantly lifted a piece of tortilla. She sat on a short tree stump with her legs stretched out, her torn feet resting over a log.

Next to Amelia were two women. One of them ground corn while the other patted tortillas and laid them gently over a hot metal sheet. A cute baby girl, about half a year older than Luisito, sat on a sarape near Abuelita. Her short hair, gathered atop her head, looked like a tiny palm tree. She was mesmerized by a pair of blue tin cups in front of her.

"How's Luisito?" asked Abuelita.

"The doctor gave him some medicine," I said. "He doesn't feel as warm anymore."

"We were on our way to see the doctor too," said Abuelita, motioning her chin toward Amelia's injured feet. "But she begged to eat first."

Marietta stole glances at Amelia and Abuelita before turning to me. "Anything else I can do for you?"

"No, gracias," I said. "We're fine."

Abuelita didn't answer. Instead, she eyed Marietta

up and down. It was obvious Marietta's way of dressing bothered her, but Marietta didn't seem to mind or care.

Marietta excused herself with a nod and walked away.

I sat on the ground next to Abuelita, and when the baby girl noticed Luisito in my arms, she dropped her tin cups and quickly toddled toward us.

"That's my daughter, Inocencia," said the woman patting the tortillas. "She goes by Chencha, and she loves babies. The funny thing is that she doesn't realize she's one herself."

I liked the name *Inocencia*. It had a gentle flow to it. Saying it made me think of something pure and beautiful. I would have like to have called her Inocencia, but it sounded much too formal for a baby.

"*Hola*, Chencha," I said and brought Luisito closer to her. Her large, intense eyes widened as she observed Luisito.

"Beh-beh?" said Chencha. "*Mimis?*"

"Yes," I said, amazed at how much she spoke. "It's a baby, and he's mimis, he's sleeping."

Chencha put her tiny index finger to her lips. "Shhhhh. Mimis."

All the women chuckled, and Chencha laughed and clapped as if she'd said the funniest joke.

"This is my fourth tortilla," said Amelia with pride.

"You better leave some food for the troops," said Abuelita.

"No worries, *Doña*," said the woman grinding the corn. "We're Pancho Villa's people. There's plenty of food here."

Dusk took over the camp and transformed it into a magical place. Objects that had littered the ground earlier became less glaring, and the small fires that burned throughout the camp came to life, like a clear sky bursting with stars.

An arroyo cut through the camp. Its walls were filled with small hollows people had dug, resembling a giant mud wasp nest. In each cranny, candlelight flickered, revealing photos, items of loved ones, and pictures of saints. The creek ran dry, but still, it carried a stream of soft amber light and murmurs filled with prayers and petitions for the living and the dead.

There was a sense of joy in the camp. Sounds of people singing, laughing, and playing guitar filled the night, and every time the mountain breeze blew, it carried the smells of beans, tortillas, chili, and roasted meat. When I asked how people could be so happy in the midst of war, I was told that life was short, especially in combat, and the chance to come together as a family and celebrate both life and death was always embraced.

It was late into the evening when Abuelita sat across a campfire and rocked Luisito. He still hadn't smiled, but at least he'd opened his eyes, eaten, and was without fever. Amelia, sitting next to them, clapped her hands to the rhythm of the music. Her bright eyes didn't seem to blink as she watched the dancing couples kick up dust in the open patch between the fires. Her bandaged feet rested on a crate and swayed side to side.

The music—filled with guitars, trumpets, and fiddles—was uplifting, and my heart skipped a beat when Papá's favorite song, "*Adiós*, Mamá Carlota," was played. The song told of the days when Mexico had fought off the French invaders and bid farewell to the unpopular French Empress Carlota. Its joyous ring let us know that together as Mexicans, we'd risen, fought, and prevailed. Papá liked the song because it'd made him feel like he too could overcome.

"Why won't you get up and dance?" asked Marietta,

standing in front of me. The glow of the fire lit half of her face.

I looked down at my bandaged feet and shook my head. "I'm too tired."

"Same reason I don't dance," said Marietta. She sat next to me on the ground. "You said you're not from this town. What brought you here?"

I told Marietta all about the Federales, about how they'd taken Papá away, burned our home, and destroyed our village.

"So, what now?" she asked. "Where do you go from here?"

"We're going north, to *el otro lado*," I said. "The other side."

Marietta looked shocked. "The United States? Why?"

"It's too dangerous here," I said. "I was told we'd be safe across el Río Bravo."

Marietta turned her gaze to the fire. She pressed her lips together and gave a subtle nod.

"Besides," I said, "I want to learn to read and write, and there aren't any schools here."

"You know who Pancho Villa is?" asked Marietta.

I nodded. Papá had told me about him. Pancho

Villa led the rebels in northern Mexico. Many folk songs called *corridos* were sung about him, his bravery, and his love for the poor. Even children's riddles mentioned him. He was loved by many, feared by many, and was known to have a weak spot for children, especially poor ones.

"Villa's opening schools everywhere," said Marietta. "He wants all kids to learn to read and write. Maybe you can go to one of his schools."

I glanced over at Luisito, who slept on Abuelita's lap, and then at Amelia, who yawned but still clapped. She swayed her bandaged feet from side to side. My family looked so peaceful and content, but how long would it last?

"How did you become a soldier?" I asked Marietta.

"It's a long story," she said.

I shrugged my shoulders, smiling.

"Where to start?" said Marietta. Her eyes locked on the campfire in front of us.

"It'd always been my papá and me," she said. "My mother died giving birth, and I had no siblings. Since my papá never remarried, he focused solely on me and taught me everything he knew." Marietta lifted her chin and her face lit up as she continued. "Papá was great. He was the best *vaquero*, cowboy, in the region. Everyone always brought horses for him to tame, and he trained them so well, you barely had to touch the reins to let the horse know what to do."

Marietta sighed, and the glow in her eyes faded. "Almost three years ago, two Federales stopped at our home. I was preparing dinner when I heard a scuffle outside. I looked out the window and saw Papá wrestling a soldier to the ground. The second federal stood next to the tussle, laughing. I ran for the door, but before opening it, I heard a gunshot. Slowly, I cracked the door open and saw my papá kneeling, holding his pistol over a dead federal. The other one, no longer laughing, pulled out his pistol and aimed it at my father. I screamed and ran toward my papá right as the federal pulled the trigger."

Marietta squeezed her eyes shut and remained quiet. The firelight burned red over her face as a lonesome trumpet blew to the song "*Las Coronelas.*" Two fiddles, with silky sounds, followed before Marietta spoke again.

"The federal had seen me," she said. "He'd heard my scream and was soon charging toward me like a rabid

ALDA P. DOBBS

dog. I ran back to the house, fast. I could feel him closing in with every step. Once inside, I ran to my room and shut the door. I grabbed a rifle from under my bed and aimed at the closed door. Within a second, the federal kicked open the door, and I fired."

Marietta looked at me with a smirk. "The fool didn't stand a chance."

"Did your papá live?" I asked.

"No, he was gone," said Marietta, holding back a sigh. "I kissed him and quickly said farewell because, over the horizon, a dust cloud was bringing more Federales my way. I grabbed as many weapons as I could, mounted my mare, and took off to the mountains."

Her story opened a pit in my stomach. I couldn't imagine losing Papá. But what if I had lost him already? Marietta's father had died in his own home, away from battlefields, away from danger. Papá, on the other hand, was out in the desert, fighting a war with a group of soldiers he detested. My body felt sick trying to think of the chances of Papá still being alive.

My gaze turned to Marietta. She looked strong despite having lost her father. For a moment, I envied her. I wanted that strength. I needed it more than ever.

"Is that where you became a captain?" I asked. "In the mountains?"

"Not right away," said Marietta, running her fingers through her short hair. "First, I pinned up my braids and disguised myself as a man because nobody ever bothers men. I then joined a group of rebels and started out as a messenger. Later, I became an explosives expert. I began fighting in battles, and before long, I led men into them. The promotions came once I proved myself on the battlefield by winning three battles."

"But everyone knows you're a woman now, right?" I whispered, leaning toward Marietta.

Marietta nodded. "After winning five battles as a captain, I unpinned my braids and let them loose. No one could believe it. But since I'd proven myself many times, they let me be. I went from *Mario* back to *Marietta* and still kept everyone's respect."

I was speechless. I wanted to be like Marietta. I wanted to learn things, to teach things. I wanted people's respect.

"Why do you fight?" I asked. "To avenge your father's death?"

"I did at first. I was outraged, but as time passed, I

remembered talks I had with my father about the injustices in our lives. We both wanted a better Mexico. A Mexico that belonged to everyone, not just the rich, and especially not the foreigners."

Marietta picked up a handful of desert dust and held it in a clenched fist in front of her. She released a thin, almost invisible trickle of sand through the bottom of her fist.

"This is how the rich have held our corn for generations," she said. "They've held it tight before our hungry mouths while denying us land and liberty. They've treated poor women like you and me worse than dogs." Marietta spread her fingers open, releasing the sand back into the desert. She dusted her hands and glanced around the camp. "This revolution is going to change everything. It's going to force open those tight fists, those shallow minds. The bloodshed will be immense, but it'll be well worth it at the end."

I hugged my knees closer to my chest and looked down at my bare feet. They glowed under the campfire. So many emotions spun inside me. How much blood would it take? I wondered. Would it take Papá's blood? My cousin Pablo's? Marietta's? I knew Papá. I knew he would have wholeheartedly agreed with Marietta. He too had a passion for a better Mexico. Unfortunately, he'd been forced to fight on the opposite side.

"You probably won't believe this," said Marietta. "But a hundred years from now, Mexico will be unrecognizable. It'll be such a rich, beautiful country that the *gringos* up north will be the ones crossing the river into Mexico for a better life."

Marietta chuckled at her own words, and I smiled, hoping there was some truth to them. She remained quiet, staring at the campfire, then at me. "Petra, what do you want in life? Deep down inside your heart, what is it you want most?"

I looked up at the sky and thought about my answer. "I want peace," I said. "I want peace for me and my family, and I want my papá back in our lives. I also want land, not much, just a small piece to live on. I want to go to school and for my sister and brother to go to school too. Someday, I want to be a teacher. But for now," I said, resting my head over my knees. "All I want is peace."

"How old are you?"

"Twelve," I said.

"Really? I thought you were about fifteen," said Marietta. "You're definitely mature. You're more mature than most soldiers here."

Marietta wasn't the only one. Most strangers often thought I was older, especially after Mamá's passing.

"I'm going to make you a deal," said Marietta.

The word *deal* struck me and reminded me of Adeline. I sat up straight, anticipating Marietta's proposal and hoping there'd be no interruptions this time.

"Join us," said Marietta.

"Join who, the rebels?"

Marietta nodded, "Yes. This army needs good, smart fighters like—"

"But I want peace," I said, raising my voice. I quickly lowered my eyes, realizing I'd been disrespectful.

"I know." Marietta nodded repeatedly. "Every soul in this camp wants peace. We're all tired of fighting, but in order to achieve peace and attain the land and freedom we want, we need to fight."

I sat quietly, and once again my heart fluttered. I pictured myself wearing pants, riding a horse, and armed to the teeth. I pictured Amelia cheering me on and next to her Abuelita, wearing a pout.

"I've never fired a pistol," I said, "or—or blown anything up."

"That's easy," said Marietta. "I'll teach you. What I have a hard time teaching is leadership."

"But I don't know anything about leadership."

"A few minutes ago, you told me what you and your family endured since your mother's passing and your father's forced conscription. You are the reason your grandmother and siblings are alive right now, Petra. You're a good leader."

I looked at the other women in the camp—the ones clapping and dancing who'd been cooking and cleaning earlier. Almost all of them wore dresses and none carried weapons like Marietta.

"I know how to cook," I said. "I can grind corn, wash—"

"No," said Marietta. "If I train you and pay you, it'll be for fighting. All your strength will go toward the revolution so that we can win. Your salary will be enough to pay for someone to cook and clean for you." Marietta looked over at the two women who had fed us earlier. They both sat on the other side of the fire, chatting with Abuelita.

"The majority of the women you see here cooking, cleaning, tending children are *soldaderas*. They're strong and brave, and as hardworking as you and me, but their calling is different."

"What kind of work would I do?"

"You can be a sharpshooter, an explosives expert—I can even teach you how to be a spy. Sometimes, I wear a dress, go over to the Federales, and act like one of their soldaderas only to gather information."

"What about my family? What happens to them if I join?"

"They could join the soldaderas. Your pay can cover their food and other expenses. We start you off at one *peso* per day, plus fifty centavos extra if we're fighting."

My heart all but stopped. I'd never made more than a single peso for an entire week of selling firewood. And Papá, the most he made at the mine was three pesos for six days of work.

"Is that not enough?" asked Marietta.

"It's—it's plenty," I said. Papá crossed my mind. Maybe I could find a way to rescue him. Maybe I could save enough money and search for him after the war.

"Think about it," said Marietta. "You don't have to

give me an answer now. Talk it over with your grandmother, and think about it some more tomorrow." Marietta stood up and dusted herself. "Tonight is our last night here. The entire camp leaves by tomorrow afternoon, but feel free to ride the train north with us. It'll give you a feel for our way of life. Once we arrive at the next station, let me know your answer."

Marietta wished me good night and walked into the darkness, fading quickly among the ghostly tree figures. I walked over to my family and lay next to them. Amelia had fallen asleep hugging the new shoes Marietta had given her, and Luisito, asleep too, wore a knit cap that sat just above his eyes. He slept next to Chencha, the baby girl who had kept us laughing all day.

The stars shined brighter as we delved into the night. I lay my drained body down, but despite my full belly, the warm fire, and the rebel sentinels keeping vigil, I could not sleep. Marietta's words had turned my mind into a busy beehive. All sorts of hopes, fears, and motivations buzzed in and out of my head. I thought about Papá, and I thought about Mamá. What would they have told me to do? Would they have encouraged me to join the cause? Or urged me to keep north?

Tomorrow would be another day, and I'd talk it all over with Amelia and Abuelita. For now, I fixed my eyes on the campfire and squeezed my baby diamond through the fabric of my skirt. And as embers took over the dying flames, the bees stopped buzzing, and my eyes sealed in hopes of a better tomorrow.

thirteen

LAS CABRAS

Early the next morning, I awoke to the smell of coffee and opened my eyes to a strange, red world. I propped myself up on one elbow and blinked at the crimson light seeping through the mesquite branches above me. I rubbed my eyes. Small clouds filled the sky, lots of them, but each puff, lined with darkness, held the color of a ripe, prickly pear—a deep bloodred.

"*Buenos días*, Petra," said Amelia. "You want some coffee?" She sat near the fire next to the old woman who'd fed us the day before. Her name was Doña Amparo. She was a small woman, but despite her age and stature, she carried herself with strength and a lot of pride.

Abuelita slapped tortillas into shape while Luz, baby

Chencha's young mother, ground corn on the metate. Not far from them, on a sarape, sat Luisito. He gnawed and drooled on a cartridge bigger than his hand while Chencha invited him to play with her tin cups.

I walked toward the fire, tightening the shawl around my shoulders and staring at the plum sky that grew fiery near the sun.

"*Ten*, m'ija," said Doña Amparo. She handed me a cup of coffee.

I sat on a log and let the coffee's warm steam soothe my face.

"Buenos días," said Marietta.

I quickly put the cup on the ground and jumped to my feet.

Marietta turned to me. "Please, sit. I'm between meetings and came here for a quick bite."

Marietta wore a small-brimmed hat and a different jacket, but the scarf around her neck was the same purple one.

Doña Amparo handed Marietta a taco and a steaming cup of coffee. Marietta drank the coffee in two quick gulps and wolfed down the taco. She turned to me as she chewed her last bite.

"We're leaving earlier than expected," she said, looking at the sky. "The repair train leaves in a couple of hours. After they depart, we need to board our train and leave before the storm comes."

I looked up at the sky and then turned to Marietta. Her gaze was on me, and my hands grabbed at my skirt to stop them from trembling. I didn't yet have an answer to her proposal.

She wiped her mouth with her hand. "Don't board the train until I get back. Wait for me here."

I agreed with her, but I could feel my heart beating fast. I wondered if Marietta wanted an answer to her proposal by then, or maybe she had a special mission planned for me.

Marietta thanked Doña Amparo for her breakfast and marched off.

"It's going to be a long day for us soldaderas," said Luz, dipping her hands into a bucket and grabbing handfuls of soaked corn. She was a pretty girl with long, slender arms, and she looked to be about seventeen or eighteen years old. She had a smile as bright as Chencha's.

"What do soldaderas do?" I asked loud enough for

Abuelita to hear. Perhaps becoming a soldadera was something that would interest her.

"People call us camp followers," said Luz. "But we're actually the backbone of this revolution."

Doña Amparo gave big nods. "If not for us, these soldiers would starve."

"Is it dangerous being a soldadera?" I asked.

"It can be," said Luz. "Sometimes I take my husband's meals into the trenches, and while he eats, I pick up his weapon and fight."

"But do you know what's more dangerous, m'ija?" Doña Amparo asked. She scratched the side of her face with her arm. "Staying back in your village is far more dangerous. When the men are gone, you're unprotected, and if the Federales show up, olvídalo. They turn your world upside down." Doña Amparo took in a deep breath as she placed a raw tortilla over the comal. "I feel a lot safer here."

"Me too," said Luz.

"Is your husband here too?" I asked Doña Amparo.

"No, m'ija. My husband and son were both killed a while back. I'm now a *madre*. I make a living by cooking and cleaning for soldiers who have no family here. I don't make much, but it's enough."

Abuelita kept her eyes on the tortillas she patted and never joined in the conversation.

Baby Chencha's efforts to play with Luisito went unnoticed, so she shifted her attention to Amelia's boots, particularly the laces.

Amelia giggled and pulled her feet back, hiding them under the sarape. Every time Chencha found them, Amelia cheered. Chencha mimicked Amelia's clapping and bounced her tiny body up and down with glee.

Amelia turned to Luz. "Does Chencha dance?"

Luz chuckled. "Chencha loves to dance, especially the Tinguiriringui dance."

Amelia cocked her head to the side. "Is that the same as the Tinguililingui dance?"

"It's the same," said Luz, wiping her hands over her apron. "Look, let me show you how *chula* Chencha looks when she dances it."

"She does," said Doña Amparo. "She looks adorable."

Amelia turned to me. "Petra, can you make Luisito dance too? Please?"

Luz and I grabbed each baby firmly by placing our hands under their arms. We sat on our haunches and stood the babies on our laps facing the audience. Both knew what was coming, especially Chencha because she began bouncing up and down long before the song started. Fortunately, Luisito was in a good mood, otherwise he'd want nothing to do with the dance.

Luz gave Chencha a big peck on the cheek. "Are we ready? Here we go," she said and began singing.

Tinguiriringui, Tinguiriri
Tinguiriringui, Tinguiriri
Tinguiriringui, Tinguiriri
Tinguiriringui, Ti

Luz and I repeated the song and dance, gently bouncing the babies up and down and side to side with matching movements. Both babies looked like a pair of marionettes that had come to life and were anxious to dance on their own. Luisito chuckled some, but Chencha's joyful squeals were probably heard beyond the camp.

It was late morning when the repair train announced its departure. By then, every single cloud had vanished and the sky's plum color had turned into a gleaming blue.

After Luz secured Chencha to her back, she, her husband, and Doña Amparo all gathered their belongings and hauled them to the train like pack mules. People by the hundreds did the same throughout the camp in a very organized way, like it'd been part of their lives forever.

Luisito had grown fussy, and when Abuelita offered to take him on a stroll, I agreed without volunteering to take him myself. I wanted time alone with Amelia. I wanted her to be the first, rather than Abuelita, to hear about my plan to join Marietta and the Revolucionarios.

I took a deep breath and walked up to Amelia. She crouched over her feet, which now wore laced boots.

"Amelia," I said, standing in front of her. "Did you like the camp?"

"I did," she said. Her fingers fumbled with the shoelaces. "I liked the food, the music, the dancing people... and baby Chencha too. She's cute."

"I..." I was out of words. Amelia was only six years old. I didn't know how she'd take my plan.

"You what?" she said, her eyes still on her laces.

"I was thinking about joining Marietta, becoming a...a soldier like her. What do you think?"

Amelia's busy fingers stopped. She looked up at me with squinting eyes. "A soldier?"

"Yes," I said with a nervous laugh. "You think I'd make a good soldier?"

Amelia sprung up. "Yes! You'll be the best soldier ever. And when you get a horse, I could help you feed him, bathe him, and I can also—"

"What are you two talking about?" said Abuelita, walking up behind me.

Amelia pushed me aside and began rambling.

"Petra's going to be a soldier," said Amelia.

Abuelita shot a stare at me.

"She's going to get a big horse, and she's going to let me feed him, bathe—"

"Amelia," I interrupted. "I said I...I—"

"You what?" said Abuelita. She handed Luisito to Amelia and glared at me.

"I..." I shut my eyes, and as I filled my lungs, I snatched every bit of courage inside me. "I want to join Marietta." There. I'd said it.

"You what? You want to join the rebels?" said

Abuelita. "What is wrong with you?" Her Spanish switched to Nahuatl, her native tongue, and I knew I was in trouble.

Abuelita had always told us about being forced to learn Spanish, about the beatings, and about people telling her that her mother tongue was a filthy language. But every time joy or anger flooded Abuelita's soul, her Nahuatl came out. I hated not understanding it. It was like observing a majestic land across a giant canyon. No matter how much I stared, I could never climb its tress, swim its rivers, or truly get to know its people.

Abuelita switched back to Spanish. "I didn't raise you to roam the streets like a dog, like that Marietta."

"Marietta's not a—"

"Marietta *está loca*," said Abuelita. "*Se le van las cabras.* She's crazy. She wears pants like a man, walks like a man—she's like a donkey without a leash. Nobody will ever marry her."

"Who cares about marriage," I said. "We're in the middle of war."

"I care!" shouted Abuelita.

Amelia and Luisito shifted their eyes between Abuelita and me.

"You're twelve years old, Petra," said Abuelita, "and next year, boys will be asking for your hand. If you follow Marietta's footsteps, no boy will want to marry you either."

I clenched my fists and bit my tongue. There was so much I wanted to say.

"A woman belongs at home, in the kitchen—cleaning, grinding corn, making tortillas—not on some battlefield," said Abuelita. She drew in her breath and sat on a tree stump. "Do you know how embarrassing it was back home to know you were climbing trees like a monkey and chopping wood? Why couldn't you be like other girls and sell tamales or tortillas?"

In Esperanzas, it'd seemed as if every poor, orphaned girl sold food and hardly made any money. If I was to keep my promise and feed my family, I had to come up with something not available at every street corner.

"You don't have a mamá," said Abuelita, "so I'm going to tell you what my mamá used to tell me. A woman's job is to take care of her man. If he scolds her, she keeps quiet. If he beats her, she bears it. Otherwise, he'll question her upbringing." Abuelita eyed me up and down. "And right now, I don't think I'm doing too good with your upbringing."

My jaw tightened, and I bit my tongue harder, tasting the blood.

"Our dire time is over," said Abuelita. "You heard Doña Amparo. Villa's people are well kept. How about we join the soldaderas instead? We could cook food, make tortillas, wash clothes, and in the meantime, you can start looking for a boy to take care of you."

Something powerful took over me, and I could no longer hold my tongue. "Who do you think's been taking care of you, and me, and the rest of us since Papá left?"

Abuelita looked both stunned and upset.

"I have," I said, hitting my chest. "And I never want to be scolded, or beaten, or kept in some kitchen. I don't need a boy to take care of me. I can do it myself just fine."

I stomped away before Abuelita could say anything.

I ran to the dry arroyo and crouched with my back against the wall full of empty crannies. I shut my eyes and pressed my fists against my face. My heart hammered inside my ears louder than the train whistle.

I considered Abuelita a wise woman, but her words and actions baffled me. Her wisdom of the desert, her closeness to it, and her stories of our ancestors always left me wanting to learn more. But how could such a wise person believe it was fine for a woman to be beaten?

I thought about my promise to Papá and what little was left of my dreams. I had no time to think about marriage. The thought alone of a husband beating me one day shot fire through my chest. Papá had never laid a finger on Mamá. Why should I expect different?

I didn't care what Abuelita thought about Marietta. Marietta was tough, and she wore pants. And with those two big pistols at her hips, only a fool would try to touch her.

I was convinced. Joining the rebels was what I had to do.

fourteen

EL ÁGUILA

Loose dirt near my feet seemed to rattle and bounce at the deafening sound of the train whistle. I was still inside the dry arroyo, still fuming over what had happened with Abuelita. And as the second whistle sounded off, I armed myself with few deep breaths and headed back to my family.

From a distance, I saw Amelia crouched over her shoes again while Abuelita bounced Luisito in her arms. Marietta stood next to them, and my face burned at the thought of what Abuelita may have told her.

Marietta, with a stoic face, rested her thumbs over the cartridge belt that wrapped around her waist.

"There you are," said Marietta. "Are you ready?"

"Sí, capitana," I said and helped Amelia up from the

ground. I glanced at Abuelita. She didn't say a word or make eye contact with Marietta or me.

I carried our stack of sarapes with one hand and held Amelia's hand with the other. Marietta walked beside me, scanning our surroundings. Abuelita, about twenty steps behind, seemed to walk slower than usual.

"Did my grandmother say anything to you?" I asked Marietta.

Marietta looked down at the dust kicked up by her boots and shook her head. "I asked her where you were, and she pointed to the arroyo. When I turned, you were coming."

Marietta and I stopped a few feet from the train and waited for Abuelita, who'd stopped to chat with some of the soldaderas.

Hundreds upon hundreds of people walked past us up a slope, toward the tracks. They carried everything they owned on their backs, their arms, and some even on their heads. They carried bundles of firewood, baskets, water jugs, crates, metates, and pails of cooked corn. Men, women, and children swarmed the train like ants on a piece of fruit. They climbed the side ladders onto the top of the boxcars. Once atop, they settled their belongings and raised short canvas tarps. Small columns of smoke rose from the tops of several boxcars.

"What's burning up there?" I asked.

"Small fires the soldaderas are lighting," said Marietta. "They'll be cooking lunch during the ride."

A group of boys gathered across from us, laughing. They surrounded a small boy and urged him to flip a tin cap.

"*Corcho o lata?*" shouted the small boy, holding the cap in the air. All bets were made, and the boys waited to see if the cap had landed on its cork lining or its tin top.

"What are they betting?" I asked.

Marietta grinned. "I think it's who gets to sleep down there." She pointed to the hammocks strapped to metal rods under the boxcars.

Amelia let go of my hand and walked behind us. She knelt on the ground near a group of boys squeezing in a last game of marbles.

While horses were pulled up ramps to board the train, men sat on top of the boxcars with their legs dangling over the edge. Each man held a rifle, a cigarette, or a guitar, but all of them sang together. Amelia's high-pitched laugh came from behind me when the

ALDA P. DOBBS

men sang a song we'd never heard before. It was about a *cucaracha*, a cockroach, and how it could no longer walk.

After Abuelita reached us, Marietta took us inside one of the cars. The stale air inside carried the smells of animals and of the exhaustion of people living day to day. Grown-ups, children, and crying babies filled the seats and most of the aisle, while dogs, goats, piglets, and birdcages filled the empty spaces. A lone chicken pecked at a cigarette butt on the floor.

We reached a long seat where a young boy sat with his arms stretched across it. He stood up as soon as he saw Marietta.

"Gracias, Gonzalo," said Marietta, tossing him a shiny coin.

The boy caught the coin in midair and smiled. "Gracias, mi capitana."

The boy walked away, and Marietta motioned with her arm, inviting us to take a seat.

"Since this is your first time riding a train, I thought I'd save you a seat inside a car," said Marietta.

"Gracias," said Abuelita, looking away.

Marietta turned to me. "If you need anything, I'll be

about ten cars ahead. Otherwise, I'll come see you in a few hours."

I nodded, and Marietta made her way outside. I looked out the cracked, tarnished window and could still make out her figure. I followed her until my eyes lost her in the crowd.

The train whistle blasted a few times, and as the big, iron wheels began to roll, the brass metal clanked in the distance. Soon we'd left the small town and found ourselves in the open desert again.

Everyone in our car rattled along as an old man played his tin flute. Men and women sang and clapped to the old man's tune and would've probably danced if given the space.

We stopped at two different stations, and each time, vendors standing on the platform rushed to the train's windows in hopes of earning a few coins. They carried baskets full of tamales, *camotes*, and pine nuts.

We exited the train at both stops to get fresh air and stretch our legs. Women, who'd been sitting inside with us, built quick, small fires to boil water for coffee. The second station we'd stopped at had a caved-in roof. Its walls, riddled with bullets, had been painted black by smoke.

It'd been about half an hour since our last stop. The next one would be our last, and Marietta would be expecting an answer to her proposal. My mind spun. Going north meant settling down, finding a good job, and pursuing my dreams. Staying in Mexico meant fighting for a cause, searching for Papá, and fulfilling my dreams once the revolution was over. But how long would the revolution last? And if the rebels won, would there be change? Would the hearts of the people holding our corn soften?

Our people had been enslaved by the Spanish for three hundred years. After Mexico won its independence the shackles were removed, but people's hearts remained the same. The rich still owned all the lands and continued to whip the poor just as before. I didn't want to remain in a place without change.

I glanced at Abuelita. She sat next to me with Luisito asleep on her lap. Amelia lay asleep at our feet over a sarape.

I took a breath to speak, but Abuelita stopped me before I could.

"Before you say anything," said Abuelita, "I want to tell you something about your papá."

I stayed silent. Abuelita kept her eyes on Luisito. She smoothed out his hair.

"Did you know that you and your papá were born during full moons? I think that explains why you're both so strong."

I didn't feel strong. I hadn't felt strong for a while.

Abuelita continued. "Your papá was born in the hacienda your cousin Pablo worked on. He was four years old when he began helping your grandpa and me in the fields."

I straightened up, listening to every word. Papá had never spoken of this. He'd always said he'd been born in the mountains.

"One day," said Abuelita, "when he was twelve, he came to me with a decision—he wanted to run away. He said he was tired of living in the hacienda, tired of the foreman always beating him." Abuelita stole a quick glance at me. "And the beatings were worse when the hacienda owners watched.

"Your papá also hated our debt to the hacienda," Abuelita continued. "He'd always say, 'Ma, these meager wages will never be enough. I don't want my children to inherit this debt or this life.'" Abuelita sighed. "But when the idea of him running away came to my ears, I put my foot down and said no."

"You said no?" Frustration quickly rose inside me. "Why?"

"Where would he go, m'ija?" said Abuelita. "Besides, God destines people to be born rich or poor, and it's His will for us to remain the same for the rest of our lives. But your papá saw things different, and a week later, he ran away to the mountains."

Why had Papá never mentioned this? Had he been ashamed about it, or had he not wanted me to run away from things like him?

Abuelita stared at Luisito, but still, I could see the tears building up in her eyes. It bothered me to see her in pain.

"My heart was crushed," said Abuelita, her voice hoarse. "Especially when the hacienda's foreman called upon the *Rurales*, the mounted police. He asked them to search for your papá and to shoot him on sight."

"But they never found him, right?" I asked.

"The years passed," said Abuelita. "The hacienda owner died, and later the foreman did too. Everyone forgot about your papá, but not me. Every day I prayed to la Virgen for his safety."

"When did he come back?" I asked.

"Ten years later. He surprised me during a village festival." Abuelita half laughed and half cried. "I couldn't stop hugging him. And that same day"—Abuelita turned to me—"I met your mamá. She was this big with you inside her belly."

I smiled, picturing Mamá and Papá together, both young.

"Your papá, even at twelve, dreamt of a better life. Just like you. Maybe joining the rebels is something you have to do," said Abuelita.

I was shocked. Did Abuelita really mean this? Was she giving me her blessing to join?

Abuelita took the end of her shawl to wipe her eyes. "I'm still scared, though. I've lost your father. I've lost Pablo." Her voice broke. "And now, the thought of losing you—" Abuelita stopped talking and hid her face under her shawl. Her small, frail body trembled as she cried without making a sound.

"Abuelita." I caressed her head. "You haven't lost any of us, and I... I'm not even sure if I want to join."

Abuelita nodded, drying up her tears. "Well, if you do join," Abuelita said between sniffs, "rest assured that you and your papá, as kids, always waited to be served. You never stuck your hand inside the pot when I turned away. That means you'll always be lucky in warfare. I truly believe that."

I didn't believe a full moon had made Papá the brave man he was or that never having stuck my hand in a pot would make me resistant to bullets. Still, I nodded and smiled.

Abuelita dozed off, and as much as I tried to join the siesta, I couldn't. I had Abuelita's blessing to join the rebels, and my belly flipped like a fish out of water as I asked myself over and over if joining them was the best thing to do. Maybe I should talk it over with Marietta, I thought, to straighten my mind.

I moved down the aisle, cautiously stepping over sleeping children and squeezing myself between nursing mothers. I heard babies cry, men snore, and people catch up on the latest gossip. I reached the front of the car relieved at not having stepped on anyone's fingers, toes, or animals.

I stepped outside, and the fresh wind blowing between the cars was a relief from the heavy, stale air inside. I reached for the next door and pulled it open.

The inside of the car resembled the one before. People, animals, cages, and belongings were all tightly packed together like kernels on a cob. I made my way across, once again, without incident, but upon reaching the next car, I noticed a padlock hanging from its boarded-up door.

I tugged on the padlock, but it remained fastened. When I leaned to the side of the train, I caught a glimpse of the car's side ladder. I decided to climb it and find a different way to get to Marietta.

I stood on the ladder with my upper body leaning over the corrugated steel top. The wind blew hard and whipped my hair against my face. Carefully, with my world rattling from side to side, I reached for the wooden plank attached to the center of the steel roof. I secured my hold, climbed up and over, and slowly came to my feet. I lifted my arms out for balance like a baby learning to walk. But people paid me no mind; they went around me as if strolling down the street.

In gentle moves, I brought my shawl over my head and wrapped it around me like the other women did. I closed my eyes and let the rush of clean, crisp air brush my face. I inhaled every bit of the wondrous wet-earth smell that flowed through me.

Behind me, the sun hovered just above the mountains and shined its last rays to the dark sky ahead. The train charged toward a giant, green cloud, toward a veil of gray streaks that fell to the ground. Thick lightning bolts branched beautifully across the cloud. They lit up the sky like fireworks, like a tribute to honor the god of rain, Tláloc.

I counted seven cars ahead of me and took my time walking. I continued to keep my elbows raised, and my heart jumped with every sudden jerk the train made.

It was a different world up on top. Despite the trains' squeaking noises and the racing wind, people carried on conversations and sang too. Some women ground corn and others cooked over small metal boxes. One man taught young boys how to clean a rifle. The raised canvas kept the wind from reaching the small fire pits and provided shelter for the sleeping babies.

Under one small tarp, I caught sight of Luz and Chencha sleeping together. Chencha's white gown and dark hair flapped gently in the wind as Luz's arms held her close. Chencha looked like a sleeping angel, and I could see why Luz had named her Inocencia.

I continued to take small steps, steadying myself

and enjoying the view of the open desert. Its colors, its scents zoomed past me, and my heart skipped as I contemplated a new adventure.

With my arms stretched open, I seemed to fly like an eagle. I felt free and in control of my destiny. It was as if everything around me—the mountains, the wind, and even the storm—hailed me for having made it this far and also screamed for me to join the cause. This was my homeland, my Mexico, and it was a beautiful and enchanting place. I wanted to fight for her. I wanted to fight to make her better.

Suddenly, a loud bang turned everyone's gaze to the front of the train.

Fire engulfed the locomotive, and explosions spewed chunks of steel into the air. The massive train twisted from the front, toppling cars one by one. Screams and sounds of metal crushing pierced the air. I turned to run.

People shoved one another, and I fell hard on my knees. I shot up. Then a violent shock jolted my body, forcing my feet away from the roof.

fifteen
EL LLANTO DE TATA

Frightful screams and horrific sounds of metal twisting and crushing came to a halt. My world went silent, and then stillness followed. It was a peace so serene, it wrapped around me like a warm blanket. Nothing ached or burned. I was part of something bigger, and nothing else mattered, not the revolution, not my promise, not my dreams. My only care was to surrender to this peace.

A low murmur, one that reminded me of butterfly wings, broke my silence. The fluttering grew, and it multiplied until it sounded like a thousand butterflies caught in a snare, all of them fighting to get away. My curiosity swelled, and the peace around me vanished like fog under the sun. The murmur became clear. It was a child's cry. It was Amelia.

A force yanked me away from the still world and tossed me into a dark shell. I heard everything—cries of sorrow and screams of horror and death—except I couldn't move.

I wanted to sit up, but I couldn't even crack my eyes open. My fingers twitched, and after a long struggle, I dug them into the soft, moist dirt. I opened my eyes, and pain surged over me. My head throbbed with every heartbeat; every breath I took was like a burning stab to my chest.

"Petra," said Amelia. Her voice told me she'd been crying. "That mesquite tree saved your life."

Amelia looked blurry to me. She pointed up, but with everything spinning, I had trouble settling my eyes on anything.

I lifted my head and caught a glimpse of Luisito sitting next to Amelia. I laid my head back down and shut my eyes.

"Where's Abuelita?" I asked.

"She went to get water for you," said Amelia. "She's coming. She's right here."

Abuelita sat next to Amelia and helped me sit up. "*Cómo estás,* m'ija? How do you feel?"

I took sips of water from the small clay jug Abuelita put to my lips. She then poured water into her cupped hand and splashed it over my face. I was immediately revived, but a burning sensation stung across my face. Instinctively, I raised my hand to stop her from splashing more water.

"I know it burns," Abuelita said. "That mesquite scratched you pretty bad." She continued to splash water on me. "Look at your arms, your legs—you look terrible."

"I was scared," said Amelia. "I thought you died."

My vision became clearer, and my world spun less.

"Are you all right?" I asked, glancing at the three of them.

"We're fine," said Abuelita. "Our car didn't topple. But what in heavens were you doing up on the roof? You could've been crushed. You're lucky you fell on this thick patch of grass."

My memory of being on the train's roof was vague, and having fallen through the mesquite tree wasn't in my mind at all. I couldn't remember much of anything, and it hurt to think. I remembered riding inside the train, talking to Abuelita, then thinking about what I'd tell Marietta.

"Marietta," I said, straightening up. "I need to find her. I need to make sure she's fine."

"You're not going anywhere," said Abuelita.

"And Luz," I said. "I saw her and baby Chencha right before the accident."

I pushed myself up and Abuelita reached to urge me back down. "*Siéntate.*"

I managed to stand despite every bone in my body aching.

"I'm fine," I said. The whirling feeling in my head had stopped, but my knees buckled. Abuelita and Amelia got a hold of me.

"I told you to stay," said Abuelita. "Marietta will come looking for us soon."

I sat back down, thinking Abuelita may be right. Still, I couldn't stay put for long knowing Marietta might need help. I stood up again.

"I'm sorry," I said. "I have to go find Marietta."

"But"—Abuelita's face was full of anguish—"you can barely stand."

"I'm fine," I said, grateful that my knees hadn't turned to rubber again. "I'll be right back. I promise."

I staggered away into the destruction. It looked like

the battlefields the soldaderas had described earlier—
thick smoke, confusion and disorder, and the pungent
smell of blood and burning flesh. People ran about
carrying lit torches and oil lamps, ready for the incom-
ing darkness. They climbed atop crushed metal and
combed through debris, shouting out names.

A shooting pain through my leg kept me from walking straight. Slowly, I was able to climb up one of the
toppled cars for a better view.

The train's engine had been obliterated, and the first
few cars lay ruined and mangled. There was no telling
which car I'd been standing on or in which one Marietta
had been riding. I climbed down and asked people if
they'd seen her. The ones who did answer simply shook
their heads.

I walked past a woman standing over a pile of smoking rubble. A small tree burned behind her. As I passed
her, I recognized her face.

"Luz!" I hollered. My heart lightened when I saw her
carrying Chencha.

In my excitement, I ran to her, anxious to see the
baby and ask if she'd seen Marietta.

I caught my breath. "How's Chencha?"

Luz looked at me with wet, swollen eyes. Chencha was in her arms, wrapped in her shawl.

I took a step closer and whispered as softly as I could, "Is Chencha all right?"

Luz lifted the tiny bundle to me, and the shawl fell away. Blood covered Chencha's charred, torn gown. And her eyes, not fully shut, had lost all their light.

My hand flew to my mouth, stopping a scream from coming out. My insides turned and twisted like the dark, gnarled trees burning around us. I closed my eyes, begging myself to wake from the nightmare. But when I opened them, I saw Luz holding Chencha to her chest, crying uncontrollably.

I wanted to embrace her, I wanted to comfort her, but I couldn't. I stood frozen. It was as if I were too afraid to touch her, too afraid to relive the pain I'd felt when I lost Mamá. All I could do was cross my arms over my stomach, grip my arms, and sob.

"I found her," shouted Doña Amparo. "She's here." She waved Luz's husband toward us. He ran up the pile of rubble and immediately wrapped his arms around Luz.

"I'm here, love. *Aquí estoy*," he said, rubbing the back

of Luz's head. His own head had been bandaged, and a large blood stain seeped through the front.

Doña Amparo's proud shoulders hung low, and when she turned to me, her eyes told me she already knew about baby Chencha.

"How's your family, Petra?" asked Doña Amparo. Her hoarse voice sounded exhausted. "Are they well?"

I nodded between sobs, turning my gaze to Luz.

Doña Amparo reached for my shoulder. "This is war, Petra." I heard her draw in her breath. "Tragedy strikes, people die. It's a sacrifice." She paused before speaking again. "We'll get through this. We'll overcome."

A sacrifice? I asked myself. A sacrifice meant surrendering something valued, something cherished for the sake of a greater good. But who decided how much we sacrificed? Who decided when to stop? Who decided it'd been enough?

After a long silence, I was able to speak.

"Have you seen Marietta?" I asked between sniffs.

Doña Amparo shook her head. "I was treating some of the wounded back there, but if I were to guess, I'd say she's farther up." She pointed to a bigger pile of rubble up front.

Doña Amparo made her way to Luz and I to Marietta.

Among the horrid confusion, bodies of men and women were pulled out of the smoldering wreckage, some still clinging to their perished young. It was a sea of disaster, a calamity full of pain and agony that seemed boundless. Women wailed, and their eerie screams pierced the heart like burning daggers. Then one sudden howl broke above them all.

It was Luz, and she yelled at the top of her lungs, over and over again, "Inocencia! Inocencia!" Her tormented screams rattled every stone in the desert.

I stumbled through the horror and shook like a leaf clinging to a tree in a violent storm. I recalled Abuelita's stories about her tata fighting for Mexico's independence. He talked about the bloodshed, about the carnage and the gore. As an old man, he recounted his stories with eyes full of tears. He said the suffering and the loss of life from those days saddened him, but what upset him the most, what disgusted him the most, was that all that blood had been spilled needlessly. The little bit of land Tata had acquired for fighting against the Spanish crown, the one he plowed and planted his hopes and dreams on, was stripped away by the government he'd fought to create. It was then handed over to a rich hacienda owner before Tata could enjoy its harvest. That's why Tata cried. He cried because they had lost so much and gained so little. And as I looked at the nightmare around me, I cried too and begged the heavens that this bloodshed would lead to something better like Marietta hoped for.

I used my shawl to wipe my face and ordered myself to stop crying. I needed to clear my head. I needed to think straight and consider the consequences of joining Marietta. I was lucky nothing had happened to my family this time, but I couldn't rely on luck always being on my side. I couldn't take that chance, not when I had a promise to fulfill.

sixteen
LA INTEGRIDAD

Dusk quickly settled in, and as I followed men with torches, my eyes scanned every corner I passed, hoping to pick up on Marietta's purple scarf. The low rumble of the approaching storm sped everyone's search.

"Petra, over here!" My heart skipped. It was Marietta's voice. I looked around and saw her sitting on the ground against a tree. She waved me over.

A man crouched over Marietta's stretched legs. His back was toward me. He was shirtless, and his tattered pants were bloodstained.

"The tourniquet is too loose," Marietta said to the man. She took a big gulp from a bottle she held. "Can you tighten it and raise it a little?"

"I can't," said the man, gripping a stick that held

the bandage together. "The bandage is too short, and it's soaked. If I take it off, I may not be able to put it back on."

The man held his hand down on Marietta's bandaged leg. He looked around, desperate. "Give me your shirt," said the man to Marietta. "I'll use the sleeves."

Marietta took another swig and put the bottle down. She reached for the top button of her shirt.

"No," I said and quickly unwrapped my shawl from my shoulders. I handed it to the man. "Use this."

The man snatched the shawl from me and tore it into long strips.

Marietta looked at me and winked. "My goodness," she said and guzzled more liquor. She wiped her mouth with her sleeve. "What happened to your face?"

I shrugged. "I think I flew through a mesquite."

"You flew?" said Marietta, smiling and shaking her head.

I looked down at the man. He wrapped Marietta's leg twice, just below the knee.

"Well, flying through a mesquite beats this." Marietta motioned her chin toward her legs.

I looked over the man's shoulder, below the area he

was wrapping. I almost fainted at the sight of Marietta's leg. A long, metal rod pierced her calf.

I pressed my hands against my mouth and turned to Marietta.

"It's not that bad. It looks worse than it feels," said Marietta. She smiled and patted the bottle next to her. "It really doesn't hurt much."

The man finished tightening the tourniquet and placed his hand over Marietta's shoulder, "I'm going to fetch the doctor. Need anything, mi capitana?"

Marietta shook her head. "I'm fine. I've got good company. Just leave the lamp here."

The man nodded and rushed away into the darkness.

"Is your family all right?" asked Marietta. She bit into her lip as she adjusted her leg.

"They're fine," I responded. "But...Luz's daughter, Chencha—" A lump in my throat wouldn't let me finish the sentence, and I felt the tears building up in my eyes.

"My God," said Marietta. Quickly, she grabbed the bottle and took a long sip as if pushing the sadness back into her belly before it could rise and pour out of her eyes.

Marietta wiped her mouth with the back of her hand and glared at the wreckage. "I say we fight and kill every one of those sons of—" Marietta stopped herself. I didn't know if it was because she'd realized she was getting emotional or because she knew Papá was one of those men she'd referred to. I cared about Papá, but I also understood Marietta. I too had grief that was turning into rage. But, like Marietta, I had to make myself think clearly.

Marietta leaned her head back against the tree. She exhaled slowly before turning her head toward me.

"*Mañana*, Petra," she said. "Tomorrow I'll teach you how to shoot."

Without saying a word, I looked at Marietta's leg and then at the chaos around us.

"I'll be fine by tomorrow," said Marietta, "and the repair crew will have us up and running in a day or two."

Marietta and I locked eyes. I wanted to help her, I wanted to join her in the fight, but now was not the time.

"What's the matter?" asked Marietta.

I knelt beside her and looked straight into her eyes. "I can't join you. Not now."

"But what about the revolution—fighting for freedom, for land?" Marietta said. "We need brave people like you to help us win this war."

"I made a promise to my papá," I said. "If I were alone, I'd join you in a heartbeat. But..." Again, I turned to the world falling apart around us. "I can't protect my family from this."

Marietta turned to the rubble that still burned. Her gaze then fell on her injured leg, and I wondered if I'd disappointed her. She remained silent as the sound of thunder grew louder.

"I understand," said Marietta, her eyes still cast down.

Part of me wished Marietta would have gotten angry or even yelled at me for not having met her expectations. Instead, she turned to me and gave me the same half smile she'd given me the day we met.

"I admire you, Petra," she said. "I admire your integrity and your compassion. And no matter where you go in life, you'll be fine because you stay true to your heart."

I noticed Marietta shiver as the first raindrops fell upon us. Among the nearby debris, I found a tattered sarape. I shook off the grass and dirt and wrapped it around her.

"Thank you," said Marietta. She looked up at the sky that rumbled and flashed. "I think it's best if you leave tonight."

"I can't outrun the Federales," I said. "Not when it's this dark, and with a storm coming." I didn't want to say it, but part of me didn't want to leave Marietta behind. Not like this.

"Follow those tracks," said Marietta. "They'll lead you to a train station about twenty or thirty minutes from here."

I clenched the sides of my skirt and looked in the direction beyond the wreckage. There was a thick darkness that even the flashing sky couldn't light up.

"There should be a train there that's heading north tonight. You won't need a ticket. It's a revolutionary train, but to get to it, you'll have to cross a train bridge."

"A train bridge?"

"A bridge meant only for trains. The crossties are not very close together, and if you're not careful, you'll fall through the gaps and into the canyon." Marietta reached for the oil lamp. "Take this. There should be enough oil to get you across."

I grabbed the lamp and remained speechless, not knowing how I'd cross the bridge with Amelia and Luisito.

"Don't be afraid," said Marietta. "Take your time

crossing it. I grew up around here and crossed it many times. Even in the dark."

"Do other people know about the train?"

Marietta shrugged. "I'm sure some men have crossed over to let the station know about the wreck. That's why you should leave now. That train will leave soon after they learn we're no longer stopping there."

I knelt beside Marietta, and without thinking, I leaned over and hugged her. "Thank you."

"You're a strong girl, Petra."

I stood up but hesitated to leave. Marietta had done so much for me. I wanted to return her kindness. "I'll take my family to America. And once they're settled, I'll come back and join you."

Marietta nodded. "I trust that you'll listen to your heart and do what's best for you and your family. But I do hope I get to see you again one day."

I was grateful to have met Marietta. Her advice and her motivating words were life lessons I'd been hungry for since Mamá and Papá's absence.

"Take this," said Marietta. She untied the purple scarf from her neck. "I want you to have it." She stretched her arm out, holding the silk scarf at the end of her fingers.

I felt the fabric between my fingertips. It was softer and smoother than I'd imagined. I pushed her hand away. "I can't."

"You're turning down my gift? It's not charity. I'm giving it to you because I like you and admire you. Besides, I've got your shawl wrapped around my leg. It's the least I can do."

I smiled and took the scarf from her. I tied it around my neck, hoping to look as tough as her.

"You look great!" said Marietta, smiling and struggling to breathe. Her pain seemed to be taking over. "Promise me you'll never quit on your dreams, no matter what."

"I promise," I said.

"If they give you any trouble when you get across the bridge, tell them I sent you. Show them the scarf." Marietta winked an eye. "Now get on out of here." She forced a smile and winced.

I walked away, leaving part of me with Marietta but gaining so much more. The strength I'd seen in her—the one I'd envied the night before—I had it. It'd been with me all along. It took meeting someone like Marietta to help me realize it.

I stopped and stole a look backward. Marietta's smile had vanished, and her eyes were fixed on her injured leg. I swallowed hard, wishing I could do more for her.

"We have to cross what?" asked Abuelita when I told her.

"A train bridge," I said, helping Abuelita strap Luisito to her back. "But we need to leave now."

"What happened to your shawl?" said Abuelita.

"I gave it to Marietta," I said. "She needed it to bandage her leg."

"Did you find baby Chencha?" asked Amelia.

I paused for a moment. We were about to step into a storm, and I didn't want Amelia to enter it with a broken heart.

"I did," I said and forced a light smile.

Amelia sighed with relief, not noticing the glance I gave Abuelita. A glance that revealed what had really happened.

Abuelita crossed herself.

I grabbed the oil lamp from the ground. "Let's go before the rain picks up."

Amelia wedged herself between Abuelita and me, giving us each a hand to hold.

The entire night sky was hidden behind a blanket of heavy clouds that growled and flashed continuously. We passed the crumbled train engine and followed the tracks beyond it, making sure we stayed between the iron rails.

With only a fingernail of a flame to guide us, I fought hard to keep my jitters at bay, and together we marched into the belly of the storm.

seventeen

LA TEMPESTAD

We'd hiked the tracks for a few minutes, and still there was no sign of the bridge. The air, heavy and damp, had suddenly picked up, moving the rumbling skies closer to us. Amid the thick darkness, I did my best to keep Amelia calm.

"I'm sure it'll be a small bridge," I said. "We'll be across before the storm comes."

No sooner had I finished speaking when big, fat drops plopped down on our heads.

"I'm not scared of the bridge," said Amelia. She clutched my hand tight. "I'm scared of seeing *la llorona*."

Abuelita crossed herself.

"No such thing," I said. I'd always believed that if the ghost of the weeping woman really existed, if there'd truly been a woman who'd drown her kids and regret it for eternity, why would she roam the rivers and snatch other children to drown?

"What about *un muerto*?" said Amelia. "Can he hurt us?"

Abuelita crossed herself again.

"No," I said. "The dead can't hurt us." I didn't believe in ghosts or evil spirits, nor did I fear the dead. In my life, it'd always been the living that brought misery. They were the ones I feared.

Bursts of lightning illuminated the sky enough for us to see the bridge ahead. Its iron frame stood tall and glowed under the flash. My grip on the oil lamp tightened. The bridge appeared much bigger than I'd imagined.

A loud humming sound cracked through the air and raised every hair on my body. *Boom!* The roar from above shook the ground and rattled our bones. Luisito screamed, and Amelia clung to me, crying. We stood a few feet from the bridge when another blast ripped across the sky. This one sliced the heavens open and brought on a downpour.

I gently peeled Amelia off me and squatted in front

of her. I kept the lamp next to my face so she could look into my eyes.

"Look at me," I said, raising my voice over the thick rain. I grabbed her quivering chin and moved her face to me. "We're going to be fine. Nothing is going to hurt you. I won't let it." I looked to our side and pointed at the bridge with the lamp. "We're about to cross that bridge, and I need you to stay calm. I need you steady."

Amelia nodded, her tears blending with the rain.

"Promise you'll stay calm?" I asked.

Amelia nodded. Her soaked hair dripped over her face. Abuelita shushed Luisito by rocking him and twisting her body side to side.

"Petra," Abuelita called.

I patted Amelia's head and went to Abuelita, who said, "Maybe we should wait to cross."

I looked back toward the train wreck. I recalled Marietta's warning about the Federales and their possible attack. Between claps of thunder, I heard the distant sound of a train's whistle. It came from the other side of the canyon. We had no choice but to cross now.

"If we wait, the train may leave us behind," I said.

I wiped the rain from my eyes and helped Abuelita

secure Luisito to her back. After a few steps, we were at the start of the bridge.

The harrowing winds blew so strong, it seemed to be raining sideways. Gusts whipped our hair into our faces and bumped us against each other. I shined the light over the bridge. The crossties looked wet and slippery. A narrow walkway parallel to the tracks had missing and broken boards and no handrails. How would we steady our feet on the bridge against this fury?

The dense rain and our lamp's small flame wouldn't allow me to see past ten steps. I didn't mind because no matter how many trees I'd climbed before, I'd never lost my fear of heights. Not being able to see the canyon's depth was probably a good thing.

Abuelita tapped my shoulder. I could barely make out her words above the pelting rain. "We're going to have to crawl," she said.

I nodded, got down on my knees, and spoke to Amelia. "Abuelita and I are going to crawl across," I shouted. "I need you to ride on my back and not let go. All right?"

Amelia squinted her eyes in the rain and nodded.

I held the lamp with one hand and put the other on

a slippery crosstie. My legs wobbled when Amelia settled her weight on me. I looked back at Abuelita. She'd raised her skirt above the knee and knotted it on the side to ease her crawling. Once on her hands and knees, she motioned her head, telling me she was ready. Soaked to the bone, we crawled down the iron tracks that glowed in the lightning.

The bridge was a ladder of wooden crossties with gaps wide enough for a person to fall through. The splinters in them snagged my skirt and dug into my hands and knees. More than ever, I wished I wore pants like Marietta, pants like the ones Pablo had given me, pants like the ones Abuelita forbade me to wear.

I kept my eyes on the crosstie in front of me and nothing else. If I looked any farther, I feared a lapse that would send Amelia and me into the deep darkness.

A blast of thunder echoed in the canyon. Amelia's legs squeezed into my sides, and her arms clamped around my neck, making it hard to breathe. Every time the wind threatened to push us over, I held on to the crosstie until my knuckles hurt. Slow as a snail, I crawled inch by inch, looking back every so often to make sure Abuelita was still behind me.

Though the rain had stopped, the strong wind kept my eyes scrunched, and when the sounds of rushing water reached my ears, I knew we were somewhere halfway. In a flash of lightning, I caught sight of the white-topped waves of the raging river. They pounded and swirled against the bridge. My arms shook at the elbows. I didn't know if it was the bridge, the cold, or my fear. Every movement was an effort. Every part of me wanted to stop. Every inch of my body wanted to scream and wake myself from this nightmare.

A sudden wind gust slammed my lamp against the rail, and then a darkness—like one that exists inside deep caves—engulfed us. I let go of the shattered lamp. The sky glowed, and I swallowed hard as I watched the lamp disappear into the angry waters.

I stretched my stiff fingers, feeling for gaps and reaching for the next crosstie. My free hand gripped the iron rail for guidance the rest of the way, until at last, my fingers dug into the muddy ground.

The wind had settled. I sat Amelia by my side, and with wobbly legs, I crawled back on the bridge to help Abuelita the rest of the way.

Abuelita collapsed on her side after reaching the

ground. "Go get help, m'ija." She gripped her bloody knees. I untied her shawl and gave Luisito to Amelia.

"Hold him," I said. "I'm going to get help."

I locked my eyes on a small, distant light and ran as fast to it as my stiff knees allowed.

Amid the dim surroundings, I made out the silhouette of the station ahead. Next to it stood a silent train, and much closer to me were the vague shapes of about five men huddled in the middle of the tracks. A lamp at their feet gave off a dull light, and the tiny, orange glows of their cigarettes moved in the air like fireflies.

I hurried my pace toward them and suddenly tripped on a crosstie. I stumbled to the ground, scraping my arms and legs against the sharp rocks.

"*Quién vive?*" shouted one of the men.

Two dark figures aimed their rifles at me.

"*Ayuda*," I begged for help while trying to catch my breath.

A man holding a rifle took slow steps toward me and repeated, "Who goes there?"

"*Gente de bien*," I cried, pushing myself to my knees. "We're good folk and we need help."

The man closest to the lamp grabbed it, and the rest followed behind him in my direction.

I squinted at the light shining over me. As I spoke, the men scanned our surroundings.

"My grandmother," I said, fighting to keep my teeth from chattering. "My grandmother and my siblings... They're by the bridge. They need help."

Some of the men looked at each other as if questioning the truth in my story. All were dressed similarly to the rebel soldiers I'd seen with Marietta.

"Where'd you come from?" asked a man, pointing his rifle at me.

My gaze shifted from the man's eyes to the end of the barrel facing me. I pulled my head back. "Our train derailed. Marietta, la capitana, told me to bring my family here and take the train. We crossed the bridge, but my grandmother can't walk anymore."

A tall man wearing a sombrero lowered the men's rifles and whispered something to one of them.

"Sí, mi capitán," said the original man and slung the rifle over his shoulder. He took off toward the train.

"Capitán," said another man to the tall one. "You think she's telling the truth?"

The tall man gave a subtle nod. "She's got Marietta's scarf. And her hands and her face speak for themselves."

I glanced at my hands. They were trembling and covered in blood.

The tall man ordered the others to go help my family, and after they rushed away, he squatted in front of me. Without smiling, he gave me a gentle gaze. "How's Marietta?"

"Not well," I said. "She was injured in the wreck."

The man sucked in his breath and glanced toward the bridge. He turned to me. "Is it bad?"

"She... She's got a big gash in her calf." The man's sorrowful eyes reached into my heart. "But... I think she'll be okay." I pushed myself up, struggling to come to my feet.

"I've got you," he said and lifted me up in his arms. He carried me up the tracks to the station and sat me on the platform next to the train. Two women soon approached me. One of them wrapped a sarape around my shoulders, and the other handed me a cup of hot coffee.

Two men carried Amelia and Abuelita toward me.

I stretched my neck. "Where's Luisito?"

Amelia pointed behind her, and out from the shadows came a man bouncing Luisito in his arms.

"He reminds me of my son back home. *Está igual de chulo que mi hijo*. He's just as handsome," said the man. He let Luisito tug at his thick mustache.

The women fed us and treated our wounds.

"Are you a soldier?" asked one woman. She wrapped a strip of fabric around my knee.

I gave her a puzzled look, and her chin pointed to the scarf around my neck.

I reached for the scarf's wet, silky ends. "No. Not yet."

"The way you got your family across that bridge," said the woman, "I bet you'll make a fine soldier one day."

I blushed, but when I recalled Marietta and her injury, my heart squeezed. I looked around for the tall man who'd asked about her.

"Where's the man who carried me here?" I asked the woman.

She glanced around. "*Sepa la bola.*" She fixed her eyes back on my knee. "Who knows? I'm a busy soldadera with no time to keep up with captains' whereabouts."

Steam poured out of the sides of the train, and on its rooftop, only silence dwelled. There were no fires, no tents, no music, no one singing, nursing, or cooking, and absolutely no one preparing for the next battle.

A man carried Abuelita to the train and led us up a set of iron steps. Amelia walked behind him, and I followed close with Luisito in my arms.

We walked down the aisle of a dark, phantom train. Empty seats abounded. The few scattered souls wore faces of gloom and sorrow. They weren't rebels. Their torn clothes and loose skin told me they'd just crossed the desert. Their eyes revealed a hunger—not for food but for safety.

Abuelita took a seat behind me. She sat sideways with her legs stretched out over the row of seats. Amelia did the same across the aisle while Luisito rested his head on my lap. The only words delivered were the thanks we gave the man who'd carried Abuelita. Afterward, we spoke no more.

The whistle blew, and the brass bell clanked before the iron beast chugged away slowly. Within moments, the gentle swaying and the wheels' *tac-tac* sounds rocked my family to sleep.

I leaned my head back and shut my eyes. They burned with exhaustion. I pressed my fingertips against my eyelids for relief as thoughts of doom festered inside my head. I imagined another train wreck or the Federales attacking Marietta or us. I envisioned us never making it north. I took a deep breath but kept my eyes closed so as to not see the grim faces around me. Was it weariness I saw in these people's eyes, or did they know something I didn't? I couldn't bring myself to ask. Instead, I laid one hand on Luisito's head and held my baby diamond in the other. I then forced my mind to memories of Papá and Mamá, memories of when we were a happy family. Dreaming of them would ease my heartaches and set my hopes for a better tomorrow.

eighteen

LA ESPERA

I **straightened up as the** train's wheels squeaked and jolted me awake. The night had turned to day, and Luisito, Amelia, and Abuelita still snoozed. I must have slept through a stop because almost every seat in the car had been taken.

Outside, gray, dreary light fell over a town with buildings taller than any in Esperanzas. I leaned toward the aisle and glanced to the front. An old man sat two seats ahead. He stared at his feet stuck out in the aisle. When he caught me looking at him, his lips broke into a half smile.

"*Ya casi llegamos,*" he said. His chin pointed outside as he let me know we were almost there.

I quickly glanced out the window and then back at him. "Is this the border, already?"

The old man gave a tired nod and said, "Ciudad Porfirio Díaz."

An old woman next to him promptly corrected him. "*Viejo*, I told you they call it Piedras Negras now."

The man shrugged at me.

I looked out and saw the town's chimney. Its towering size and dark color reminded me of the one at the mine in Esperanzas. The town's name made sense. It'd been changed to Piedras Negras to honor the black stones beneath its surface—its coal. I thought the name also praised the grueling work miners poured into plucking the precious rocks from the earth. I liked the name. It was far better than Porfirio Díaz—the name of a dictator who'd refused to bring change to the poor.

The train slowed to a stop, and as it hissed, men and women gathered their belongings and gently woke their sleepy young ones. I put Luisito over my shoulder and crossed the aisle to wake Amelia up. From her window, I caught sight of the widest river I'd ever seen: el Río Bravo. America lay on the other side. My heart swelled with joy. A life of peace was a river's width away. We'd soon be out of the claws of the revolution.

Abuelita struggled to walk down the aisle and

grabbed my shoulder. Amelia followed close behind us. We exited the car, and at the top of the iron steps we stopped, bewildered.

We eyeballed hundreds of people in front of us, to the right and left, and as far as the eye could see. Everyone looked hungry, desperate, and lost.

"*Hay harta gente*," said Abuelita. "There are a ton of people, and everyone's walking in different directions."

Amelia tugged at my skirt. "Where do we go now?"

Most of the people leaving the train pushed through the crowd and walked away from the station, toward the river.

"Let's follow those people," I said. "I bet they're heading to the bridge."

We climbed down the steps and wedged ourselves in the swarm.

I squeezed Amelia's hand. "Don't let go, all right?"

"I won't," said Amelia.

We inched our way through the flock and rubbed elbows with well-dressed people and others wearing ragged clothes like ours. Smells of dirt, must, and sweat filled the narrow gaps between us. People stretched their necks, attempting to look ahead, every one of us itching for more space.

Slowly, the crowd cut around the train station and reached a wide street. Suddenly everyone had enough room to walk an arm's length from one another.

We walked past a two-story, redbrick building. Its bright-white picket fence matched its thin columns and balcony rails. I counted at least eight chimneys on its rooftop. From its balcony, men and women dressed in fancy suits and silks watched the throngs of people. Their faces were filled with worry and puzzlement.

"What's on the other side of the bridge?" asked Amelia.

"*Estados Unidos*," said Abuelita with a bright face. "That's where the *Americanos* live."

"Is it pretty there?" asked Amelia.

"I've never been there," said Abuelita. "But I've heard the streets are made of gold, and that some are even covered in diamonds."

Amelia's mouth dropped open. "Really? Is it true, Petra?"

"That's what people say." I squeezed Amelia's hand. "We'll find out today."

"Look at that building," said Amelia. She pointed to a stone building with too many windows to count. The windows stretched taller than me and were curved at the top. The structure had thick, white columns, railings, and decorative figurines. Its pale walls contrasted the dark, gray sky. It was a palace.

"Imagine living in a place like that," said Abuelita.

If the streets in America were paved in gold, I thought, maybe every house looked like that too.

Luisito remained asleep in my arms, and when I used my shoulder to scratch my chin, I smelled my damp clothes. I'd hoped for the sun to come out and dry them. Instead, it remained hidden behind clouds that threatened more rain.

Beautiful buildings surrounded us, but the mud-filled streets were the same as back home. Everyone, barefoot or not, marched right through the murky puddles in hopes of soon stepping on diamond-covered streets.

The crowd in front of us split at the end of the block. Some turned left, others right, and some remained straight.

"Which way should we go?" asked Abuelita.

I paused at the intersection and looked right, hoping to catch a glimpse of the bridge.

"I don't see a bridge," I said.

At the corner, a man sat on an upside-down crate. He carried an infant in his arms. In front of him, across a spread sarape, lay household items such as tin cups, earthenware, and a lamp.

"*Perdón*, señor," I said, approaching him. "Could you please—"

"You want to know how much this costs?" The man picked up a tin cup. Hope flooded his eyes.

"No, señor," I said in the gentlest voice. "I... I'm sorry, I just—"

"I'll give you a good price," said the man. "Please, my son hasn't eaten much in two days."

Stunned, I uttered, "Two days?" I glanced at the crowd and then back at him. "Why haven't you crossed to America?"

"I don't have money to feed my son," said the man, "much less to cross the bridge."

My stomach knotted.

"How much are they charging?" asked Abuelita.

"I've crossed that bridge many times," said the man. "It's always been one centavo. Now they're charging five centavos per head, including children. *Imagínese?*"

Abuelita and I looked at each other. Five centavos per person meant we'd need twenty centavos to get all of us across—about two days' worth of earnings from selling wood.

"How much do you have, m'ija?" Abuelita asked me.

"I only have twelve," I said.

"Twelve Mexican centavos?" asked the man.

I looked at him, baffled. "What do you mean?"

"Americans use different coins. They call their centavos *pennies*. One penny is worth two Mexican centavos. So for all four of you to cross, you'd need forty Mexican centavos."

The word *forty* sucked the air out of me. It hammered inside my head and down my gut. Why would they charge so much to the people who could least afford it?

"Where's the bridge?" I asked in a somber voice.

The man turned to look at the slow-moving crowd. "The street we're on is Zaragoza. If you follow it for about eight or nine blocks, you'll see the plaza. City hall is on the next block and the street between them is Juarez. If you make a right on Juarez, it'll take you *derechito al puente*, straight to the bridge." The man switched the infant from his arms to his shoulder. "You should go. Maybe the tariff's been lowered."

"Gracias," I said to the man, and before walking away, I pulled two coins out of my pocket. "*Tenga,* señor."

"No, m'ija," he said. "Your family needs it as much as I do. God will provide."

I hesitated, then placed the coins back in my pocket.

We continued on our path down the street, and I prayed that the fare had gone down. The street had narrowed to almost half its width, and again we were shoulder to shoulder with other people. Young, old, rich, and poor, we all shuffled along. The well-to-do rode in automobiles or fancy buggies packed with colorful suitcases and chests. The poor rode on donkeys or old carts packed with crates, cages, and sarapes. The poorest of the poor were on foot and carried all they had on their backs and their heads. Then there were people like us— the lucky ones. We were the ones who'd cheated death and had escaped with only the tattered clothes on our backs.

Automobiles, carts, buggies, and even donkeys formed a line down the middle of the street that didn't move. Those of us on foot continued to drag along the sidewalks, through and around the gaps in the line. Suddenly, the crowd came to a stop. People shouted and hissed as confusion took over.

"What happened?" asked Amelia. "Why did everyone stop?"

I tiptoed and stretched my neck to see farther. "I don't know."

I handed Luisito to Abuelita, which awoke him.

"Eh-ta," he screamed and stretched his arms to me.

"Stay here," I said. "I'm going to see what's happening."

I muscled my way through the commotion, toward the bridge, and caught a glimpse of a large building ahead. A short clock tower rose from its rooftop's center. After spotting the plaza, I realized the clock tower building was city hall. I followed the crowd's path as it curved to the right on Juarez Street, and when it became impossible to go farther, I climbed up one of the two tall pillars that guarded an arched entry. The pillars rose about a foot higher than the average man, and once on top, I could see above everyone.

I glanced toward the river. The street sloped down, and ahead, at the end of the next block, stood a tall, rectangular steel frame. Its dark iron pieces webbed and formed a tunnel over a walkway. It was the bridge. Half of it was packed with people, carriages, and animals. The other half, the American side, appeared empty. I looked across the street from where I stood, to the plaza. Its sidewalks, benches, gazebo, and dirt patches were overflowing with people. I looked back to where the streets converged. Each was a massive river of people, stagnant and desperate to flow.

I inched my way back to Abuelita, disillusioned. I observed the people I passed. I noticed their colorless lips and the dark puffs beneath their eyes. Both rich and poor had the same exhaustion, confusion, and fear that only war brings. People vented their sorrows and frustrations to each other and to the sky. A voice from a woman sitting atop an old carriage made me turn.

"When did they shut the border?" asked the woman. She wore faded silks and sat next to a heavy man.

"Just now, I reckon," replied a woman on the ground. She was barefoot with a child strapped to her back.

"Did they say why?" asked the woman on the cart.

The peasant woman shrugged her shoulders. "I was told that the Federales were no longer a threat."

"No longer a threat?" shouted the heavy man up on the cart before letting out a fake laugh. "You see those barracks?" He pointed to the pillar I'd climbed minutes ago. "It's practically empty of Revolucionarios. If the Federales showed up at this moment, we'd be at their mercy because most of the rebels are gone. Of course the Federales are still a threat."

I rubbed my hands together and stepped forward. "Excuse me, did they say when the border will open again?"

The barefoot woman sighed and shook her head. "There's an iron gate at the bridge. It's shut, and the American soldiers are guarding it. It doesn't look like they're opening it anytime soon." The woman tightened her shawl and continued her way opposite to everyone else. Soon, I noticed many others like her headed the same way, walking with shoulders dropped and faces full of despair.

"The border's been shut," I told Abuelita.

She closed her eyes and crossed herself.

Amelia looked at us, spooked. "What does that mean?"

"It means we'll have to wait," said Abuelita.

I plopped myself on the sidewalk next to Amelia. My elbows rested on my knees, and my hands pressed hard against my face. Four words swirled inside my head over and over: *border, shut, rebels,* and *gone.* My eyes grew moist, but I made sure to keep them hidden. I didn't want Amelia to see them wet. She'd think I was afraid, and I wasn't. I was exhausted. I was tired of the desert, tired of running away from the Federales. But most of all, I was tired of working so hard to keep my promise to Papá. My vow to keep my family safe was taking a toll on my body and soul.

There was nowhere to run now. It didn't matter how much the streets in America were sprinkled with diamonds; if the Federales came to Piedras Negras, everything—my family, my promise, and my dreams— would be doomed.

nineteen

EL ENCUENTRO

Luisito screamed with the same irritation that stewed inside me.

"Petra," said Abuelita. "*El niño tiene hambre.*" Luisito's wailing was out of hunger.

Discreetly, I rubbed my eyes and nose against my upper arm and cleared my throat. "Let's go to the square first. We need to stay close to the bridge in case it opens."

Word had spread that the border was closed, and the packed streets soon thinned out. As we walked, we bumped into people walking against us, away from the bridge. The line of carts and buggies that occupied the center of the street remained at a standstill.

We reached the plaza and crossed the street to the

barracks. Through its shattered windows, I could see two rebel soldiers talking to another one sitting at a small table. Once again, I climbed atop one of its entry pillars and helped Amelia climb up too. She grabbed on to the arched stone entrance and steadied herself.

"You see the bridge?" I said.

Amelia tiptoed. "I do," she said. "And I see the river too."

"That's the bridge we're waiting on to be opened," I said.

"Why can't we just swim across the river?" asked Amelia.

"You don't know how to swim," I said.

"You do," said Amelia. "I can ride on your back."

"They call it el Río Bravo for a reason," said Abuelita from below. She bounced Luisito in her arms. "That river is angry, and it's known to be tricky too. A woman I once knew lost her two sons trying to cross it, both good swimmers."

Luisito had stopped wailing, but he rubbed his red, swollen eyes nonstop. I climbed off the pillar and then helped Amelia come down.

"I'll go search for food," I said to Abuelita. "If the bridge opens, use these coins to cross." I handed her all twelve centavos.

"No." Abuelita handed me back three coins. "Let's split it even."

"What if they charge four centavos per person?" I said. "These twelve would get you all across."

"If that's the case," said Abuelita, "we'll wait for you and figure it out."

Abuelita wouldn't change her mind.

"Besides, you may need the money to buy food," Abuelita added.

I glanced around. "I haven't seen anyone selling food, but I'll see what I can find."

"Can I go with you?" asked Amelia.

"No, I want you to do this instead." I stooped in front of Amelia. "*Ponte águila.* Your eyes are better than Abuelita's. They're like eagle's eyes. If you see or hear the bridge being opened, I want you to grab Abuelita and Luisito and run across. You got me?"

Amelia frowned. "What about you?"

"I'll cross as soon as I can," I said. "We'll meet up on one of those golden streets."

Amelia glanced toward the bridge, then back at me. "I can't do it." Her voice was full of uneasiness.

"Sure you can," I said. "You're the fastest six-year-old I know."

"I know I can run fast," said Amelia, "but I can't leave you here."

"It's all right, m'ija," said Abuelita. "Petra will be back in time." Abuelita turned her back to Amelia and glared at me with worried eyes. She whispered, "Don't go too far."

"I won't," I said and walked away.

People moved around aimlessly, trying to figure out what to do next. Despite the thousands of souls roaming the streets, Piedras Negras was a ghost town. The city hall building, like the barracks, had most of its windows shattered, with a few rebel soldiers stirring inside. Across the street, a clean padlock hung between the church's wooden doors, and the wooden panels on boarded-up shops and homes still carried the smell of fresh pine. It was as if the town had recently been abandoned.

Not having found anything to eat, I walked until I'd reached the edge of town. Homes became more scattered and farmlands more visible. As the sky cracked a low growl, my heart pounded a little harder. I reminded myself I was less than six streets away from my family.

Ahead, atop a small hill, sat a big, yellow house with an odd-looking roof. Upon closer inspection I noticed that the roof, sloped like a mountain peak, had thin, dark-brown squares covering it. It differed from the nearly flat roofs in Esperanzas. The house, though beautiful, was made out of wood, and its windows and doors had also been boarded up. A covered porch wrapped around the exterior and creaked under my bare feet. I followed it to the back and found a barrel near the door.

Thankful water hadn't flooded it, I used a long branch to pick through the litter inside. An intense whiff of ripe bananas came to me. I dug deeper, quickly pulling out scraps of cardboard, fabric, and glass bottles, until finally, I saw it—a batch of bananas so ripe, the peels had blackened.

I tossed the branch and lifted the batch out of the barrel. I counted six black bananas, and when I grabbed one, its mushy meat seeped out of the folds of its peel. Frantically, I ate the squishy fruit off of my hand and licked every finger, making sure nothing was left behind.

As I wiped my hand over my damp skirt, I caught

sight of the town below me. My eyes followed the packed streets up to the bridge, which looked the same: people camped on the Mexican side, while the American side continued to appear empty. A red-and-white striped flag with a hint of blue waved at the end of the bridge. Beyond it, the grass, the trees, the bushes—it all looked greener across the river. I narrowed my eyes at the American streets. They seemed to glisten despite the gray sky both countries shared.

I cradled the batch of bananas in my arms like a newborn baby and rushed away. I couldn't wait to see Amelia's face when she saw them. I dashed down the muddy paths headed for town, cutting between two empty huts and turning a corner. I then came to a complete, sudden stop.

A group of women soldiers rode their horses up the hill, toward me. Each wore the uniform of the Federales. I froze. I knew I'd been seen. It was too late to run, too late to hide.

twenty
UNA FORTUNA

The horses trotted past me, but one woman fell out of the group. She rode back to me, holding the reins with one hand and placing the other over the big pistol on her hip. My heart hammered inside my chest. I'd heard and seen atrocities waged by the Federales against civilians. I dared not move.

The woman glanced at my purple scarf and then looked me dead in the eye. Her glare made the hairs on my forearms stand up.

"I want you to tell the people down there that the Federales are on their way," said the woman. Her horse paced around me, and though my eyes tried to follow it, I kept my head still.

"Tell them that we will show no mercy," she

continued. "Every rebel will be slaughtered and anyone trying to run to the other side will be slain." The horse circled once more before the woman kicked its sides and made it trot toward the group.

I stood motionless, too frightened to move. I was afraid that if I moved too fast, I'd be shot. Slowly, I turned my head and saw the group riding off into the desert.

I looked down at the bananas. Like a vise, my arms had squeezed them, smearing the mushy fruit on my blouse. I dashed toward the plaza, trying not to squeeze what little fruit I had left.

Abuelita, sitting on the sidewalk, flung her arms around me after I told her about my encounter. "Thank God they didn't do anything to you."

"Right after you left," Abuelita continued, "a rebel officer gave a speech to us here in the square. He stood at the gazebo and said that the few remaining rebels would soon leave the city but would return in a few days."

"What about the Federales?" I asked. "Did he say anything about them?"

"He said the Federales wouldn't be here until two or three days from now. He also said the border had been shut because of a smallpox scare." Abuelita crossed herself. "I pray to God it opens before the Federales get here."

I handed Amelia a banana. Her face wasn't as happy as I'd hoped. She had round, worried eyes as she chewed.

Luisito grabbed a piece of banana from my fingers.

"Did the officer say why the rebels were leaving?" I asked.

"He didn't," said Abuelita and then turned to me with a hopeful face. "But he urged everyone to remain loyal to the rebel cause and promised to fight the Federales to the end."

I reached for my scarf and thought about Marietta. Maybe once we crossed the bridge and once my family was safe and settled in America, I could join the cause. I could fight along with Marietta and learn to read once the revolution was over.

A man down the street near the bridge yelled in our direction. "Pepe!" He waived his straw hat high. "*El puente...está abierto.*"

The bridge had opened. I stood and picked Luisito up. "Vamos," I said to Abuelita and helped her stand. Amelia dashed ahead of us.

"Amelia," I shouted as people around us headed for the bridge. "Wait up."

Like us, everyone gathered their children and belongings and headed for the other side, only to collide with people yelling that the bridge hadn't opened. We all looked at each other with muddled eyes. Confusion continued as people dashed in different directions, some arguing among themselves or calling out for others.

Abuelita reached out to a woman walking past us, away from the bridge. "Did the bridge open?" Abuelita asked her.

The woman shrugged, looking back. "I don't know," she said. "I'm looking for my son."

An old man dragged his feet away from the commotion, toward me. He was skin and bones. His wool suit, full of holes and patches, had probably once been brown or gray. He carried a small wooden case and nothing else.

"*Disculpe*, señor," I said to him. "Did the bridge open?"

He paused, looked back to the bridge, and let out a heavy sigh. "It's open, all right." He switched his small case to his other hand and stretched out his fingers. "They're charging a fortune to cross."

Abuelita gently pushed me aside. "How much are they charging?"

"Five dollars," said the old man.

Abuelita looked like she'd been hit in the gut. She shut her eyes and brought her hand over them as if she'd been told someone dear to her had passed.

"How much is that?" I asked Abuelita, but she remained silent.

The old man spoke. "That's ten pesos."

I pulled my head back. Ten pesos *was* a fortune. In my entire life, I'd never seen a single peso, much less ten, but still, I had to ask. "Ten pesos per person?"

The old man chuckled. "Does it matter?"

I looked around. "It... It does. Maybe I can work or—"

"It's ten pesos per person," he said, eyeing the automobiles that honked at the crowds. The drivers yelled for the people to open a path as they drove around old carts and donkeys toward the bridge.

Abuelita finally spoke with a broken voice. "It would cost forty pesos for us to cross."

I felt a hole in the pit of my stomach. The fare had increased a hundredfold, from forty centavos to forty pesos. I swallowed the knot in my throat as I watched the parade of automobiles. The women sitting next to the drivers fanned themselves as their distressed faces showed a glimpse of relief.

"We'll wait," said Abuelita. Her shoulders hung as she stared at the passing automobiles.

I puffed my cheeks with air and slowly exhaled. "We have time," I said. "We have two or three days before the Federales get here, right?"

Abuelita and the old man glanced at each other. Neither said a word nor agreed with me.

twenty-one

ALEJANDRA

By late afternoon, the sky had grown darker than usual, and when nightfall came, the sky split open, and everyone scrambled for shelter. Abuelita and I spent the night sleeping on the sidewalk with hundreds of others under a torrent of rain. A family across from us let Amelia and Luisito sleep under their cart along with their children.

In the middle of the night, two blasts startled me awake. I sat up, shaken, and saw others still sleeping. I wondered if it'd been a nightmare, until a third blast went off.

Others around me sprang up with the same dazed look. Behind me, a few steps back, sat the old man. His wooden case rested atop a windowsill. He appeared calm as he stared at the sky colored red by fires near the edge of the city.

"It's the last of the Revolucionarios leaving Piedras Negras," he said. "They're burning everything before the Federales get here."

"What are they burning?" I asked.

"Bridges, mines—anything the Federales can use."

Between blasts, the snorting and grunting of horses caught my attention. About twenty steps from me, under the misty rain, I saw the shadows of six horses and a man standing among them. He hushed the animals and patted their forelocks. The figures of five men with sombreros and crisscrossed cartridge belts walked out of the barracks and joined the horses. In the glow of their lamps, they whispered to each other and loaded their horses with rifles, satchels, and canvas bags, which appeared heavy.

Two of the men left their lamps on the ground, and after they'd all mounted, they rode away into the darkness.

"There they go," whispered the old man. "The last rebels are gone." He shook his head and gave a long sigh of defeat.

With the rebels gone, we were as vulnerable as in

the desert, only this time we were trapped. At least the desert was open, and its vastness gave us opportunities to outrun the Federales. Not here. With a border as impenetrable as this one, we were doomed.

My eyes wandered, and I sensed the dread in all of us—in our breathing, in our whimpers, and on the blank stares women had while nursing their babies.

The old man reached for his case, and without a hurry, he walked up to the lamps left on the ground by the rebels.

Only scattered drops fell from the sky, and the murmur of whispers and prayers filled the night. Children tried to go back to sleep while most of the grown-ups sat up with frightened faces. I turned to Abuelita. She sat on her haunches with her eyes closed and held her hands up in prayer. I closed my eyes to pray when I heard two distinct clicks.

It was the old man. He had snapped the brass fasteners on his case open, and as he squatted in front of it, he took out a crumpled hat and a fiddle.

The old man stood up, placed the hat over his head, and positioned the fiddle under his chin. He took a deep breath and began to play.

My heart leaped when I recognized the song. It was Abuelita's favorite tune. She hummed it almost every day following town festivals. It was a waltz called "Alejandra."

I snapped my head to Abuelita. "It's Alejan—" I stopped myself.

Abuelita hid her face behind her hands. Her frail body trembled. All I could do was throw my arms around her.

"It's all right," I said, rubbing her hair back. "The Federales won't be here for another few days. We have time."

She grabbed at my blouse, pressed her face against my shoulder, and wailed.

I squeezed her tighter, hoping to bring calm and feeling helpless that I couldn't do more. Around us, men and women sobbed. One brave couple stood up with frightened smiles and began to waltz in the light drizzle. The lamps' amber glow draped over them while the old man, who'd rested his bow briefly, used a finger to pick at the strings. Each pluck matched the drops falling around us.

Despite the beautiful music and the couple dancing,

people shed more and more tears. They wept just like on the night when the smoking star had crossed our sky. Despite the tears around me then and now, I didn't believe this was the end or that this would be our last song.

The waltz came to an end, and almost everyone lay back down on the hard sidewalk. Whimpers continued to disturb the silence of the night, and as I placed one hand under my head, I stroked my baby diamond with the other. I kept it stowed away inside my pocket, afraid of losing it in the darkness. With my eyes fixed on the red sky, I squeezed the stone harder than ever. The rebels were gone. The ruined bridges and mines would buy us some time free from the Federales. But how much time, nobody knew.

twenty-two
OJOS DE VÍBORA

The next day started off quiet as people sat around waiting for news. Clouds hung heavy above us, dark and uncertain as our day.

Amelia and Luisito had finished the last of the bananas.

"I'm going to search for more food," I said as I stood up from the sidewalk.

Abuelita looked up at me. "Where're you going?"

"Not far," I said.

"You should stay close," said Abuelita.

"Yes," said Amelia. She wiped Luisito's mouth with her blouse. "What if the Federales get here?"

"I won't go far," I said. "I promise."

Abuelita nodded with a sigh. "Be careful, m'ija." She motioned me to lower myself for a blessing.

The day full of uncertainty weighed on me like a ton of coals. I dragged my feet down the muddy path, every step as heavy as my heart. I'd walked without counting the streets, and suddenly I found myself at the edge of town again.

To my right, in the middle of a field, stood a large, two-story building. Its sad, gray stone walls matched its broken picket fence. Three giant archways on the bottom floor invited me to step in.

I walked through the center archway, and the sky's low growl grew louder inside the covered courtyard. The building appeared cold and abandoned, and a gust of wind slammed a door shut behind me.

I swallowed hard and approached the door, convincing myself it'd been the wind. Slowly, I turned the knob and pushed it open.

Rows of small tables filled the room. Each had its own small chair behind it. All the rows were straight except in the far corner. Around the room, attached to the walls, were dark boards that resembled giant slates. Above them hung pictures of plants, flowers, and the human body, all with lines and curvy letters pointing to different parts. My heart almost burst with excitement—I'd stepped inside a school.

I slipped into the nearest seat and, for a moment, pretended to be a student. I straightened my back and looked attentively at the blackboard in front. Row after row of beautifully written words stretched across it. The lure to touch them was just too much.

I stepped up to the giant slate and stared at the enchanting hooks and curves. My finger traced over each letter, lifting a swarm of white dust into the air. My nose itched as excitement rushed through me.

My finger reached the end of the writing, and in my chest, I had the same satisfied feeling as if I'd eaten a full meal. I dusted off my hands and stepped back to observe my tracing when a sharp pain shot through the bottom of my foot.

I hobbled toward the board and leaned against it. From the bottom of my foot, I pulled out a thick shard of glass. I wiped the blood off my foot with the bottom of my skirt and noticed a trail of broken glass. My eyes followed it to a pile of ashes where something wooden and square lay beneath.

I limped to the pile and dug out a charred frame. Ashes blew into the air as I shook it. Slowly, I removed the remaining broken glass and used my blouse to wipe off the soot. Soon a portrait of a military man came into view.

The man wore a dark uniform. His embroidered collar and cuffs, the fringes falling from his shoulder pieces, and the numerous medals pinned to his chest and hanging from his neck told me he was someone important. He stood straight with a sword on his side. A gloved hand rested over a feathered hat next to him. My eyes swept up to his face. The man barely had a mustache or hair on his head. The ends of his mouth curled down as if in anger, and his eyes, narrowing behind perfectly round spectacles, looked like those of a rabid dog.

I almost dropped the picture. I'd never met this man before, or even seen his portrait, but I knew who he was. He was the man Papá had referred to as *el pelón con ojos de víbora*—the bald man with snake eyes. He was General Victoriano Huerta: our president and commander of the Federales. He was the traitor who'd turned this country on its head.

I tossed the picture back into the ashes. The pain from the embedded glass and from having seen the portrait sucked all the excitement out of me. My stomach rumbled almost as loudly as the thunder outside. Nauseous,

I looked around the classroom. Images of Papá being dragged away, of cut ropes hanging from trees, and of Marietta with the embedded rod came to me.

I walked down the row of seats and let my hand stroke each one. I wondered if they'd ever be filled again. Maybe once the war ended. And when it ended, who would fill them? Would it be children of the rich, or of peasants and coal miners?

I stopped for a moment, shut my eyes, and made a promise to myself. I would go to school one day, no matter what. Maybe during or after the war. Maybe in Mexico or the United States—but I was determined. And I would fight for this promise as much as I'd fought to keep Papá's.

I opened my eyes and glimpsed a piece of paper sticking out from under a desktop. I tugged on it. To my surprise, the desktop was a lid to a big storage box. I swung the top open and rummaged through what looked like a bird's nest. There was crumbled paper, broken slate pencils, dry leaves, and shiny rocks. The smell of apples hit my nose. My hand scoured faster until something moist stuck to my hand. It was a dark-brown apple core without much meat on it. I nibbled all I could from it and tossed it. I ran to the next desk and flipped it open. Nothing but papers. I went to another and then another and searched every desk in all the rooms of the building. In the end, I had four apple cores, one bitten apple, two whole apples, and a paper cone half-filled with pine nuts.

I ran down the stairs and away from the building with my small treasure tucked under my blouse. Above me, the dark skies began to open, letting through warm rays of hope.

twenty-three
HUITZILOPOCHTLI

I walked with my face raised to the sky. I closed my eyes for a moment and let the warm light pour over me. Papá had always referred to the sun as *la cobija de los pobres*, but as snug and cozy as it was, its warmth wasn't enough to blanket out my fears of what may come.

Perhaps I shouldn't go back to my family just yet, I told myself. *Perhaps I should go elsewhere to find more food.* The apples and pine nuts I'd found would only last a day at most, and tomorrow, with the Federales nearing Piedras Negras, Abuelita would likely not let me leave her side.

My mind churned, thinking of places where I might find food, when suddenly something buzzed near my face. I stopped, opened my eyes, and instinctively, swatted the small pest away. The determined critter zoomed at me again. I pulled my head back, not wanting to get stung by the big bumblebee. The creature zigzagged around me and then stopped and hovered in front of my face. There, the sunrays hit it perfectly, bringing into view its glistening feathered chest. It was a tiny hummingbird with bright-purple feathers that matched my scarf. I smiled at the tiny bird.

"Huitzilopochtli," I whispered to it. "That's what Abuelita calls you—the hummingbird of the south."

I continued to walk, looking down every cross street and hoping to spot a new place to scour. The hummingbird, though, was persistent. It continued to seek me. It zigzagged forward and back and around me as if urging me to follow it.

"Where are you trying to lead me?" I asked. For a moment, a strange feeling tugged at my heart; it pushed me to heed Abuelita's advice. Without giving a second thought, I let nature be my guide.

The tiny bird flew, and I followed its track. It stopped on windowsills and iron bars for short breaks before pressing on. To my surprise, it led me all the way back to my family and then quickly disappeared above the crowd.

I handed Abuelita the small treasure I'd found. Not

far from us, the old man who'd played the fiddle talked to a group of older boys.

"The rebels blew up everything," said one of the boys. "There's no way the Federales will show up today or tomorrow."

The old man sat on the ground. He gently stroked his case. "Last night was our final evening; that's why I played."

One of the boys laughed. "You might know how to play your fancy fiddle, old man, but I don't think you know any military stuff."

The old man shrugged, cocking his head to the side.

Abuelita handed Amelia an apple. "Take this to the man, and thank him for having played his fiddle last night."

Amelia ran to the man, and after exchanging a few words with him, she came back with a concerned look.

"What did he say to you?" asked Abuelita.

Amelia scrunched her shoulders. "He thanked me and asked if I'd liked his music. I told him I was asleep when he played and if he could play it again for me, but he didn't answer. I think he wanted to cry but didn't want me to see him."

Amelia sat next to me. Her chin quivered as she stared at the man.

"Everything's going to be fine, Amelia," I said. "You know why?"

Amelia turned to me without speaking.

"I saw a hummingbird today," I said. "Do you remember the story of Huitzilopochtli?"

Amelia shook her head.

"Huitzilopochtli is the most powerful of all the gods," I said. "He built Tenochtitlan, our empire. He also lords over the sun and war, and that makes him a good omen."

Abuelita's stories about Huitzilopochtli flashed in my head. One was that when warriors were killed in battle, they reincarnated as hummingbirds. Papá came to my mind, and I stopped myself from telling that story. Instead, I told her how Huitzilopochtli honored women.

"When women die giving birth," I continued, "Huitzilopochtli sends their soul back to earth as hummingbirds, to honor them and their sacrifice."

"Like Mamá?" Amelia uttered.

I nodded with a smile. "That bird was Mamá watching after us, telling us everything is going to be fine."

A wave of relief swept over Amelia's face. The small twinkle in her eye was like sunshine after the threat of a storm. For a moment, I envied her. I too wanted to believe. I wanted to believe everything would be fine. I wanted to believe that Mamá was that bird and that she really was... I took a deep breath. Maybe it was just a bird attracted to the smell of bananas radiating from my blouse. Either way, Mexico was a disaster, and America was out of reach. A bird that small could never fix such a big mess.

Amelia hooked her arm around mine and snuggled against me. "Te quiero mucho."

"I love you too," I said.

Suddenly, behind us, a group of men raced down the street.

One of them held down his hat. "Los Federales"—he pointed to the hill behind him—"they're coming."

My breathing stopped. I narrowed my eyes on the hill, not wanting to believe what I saw.

twenty-four
EL ADIÓS

At the top of the hill was a line of horses mounted by uniformed men watching over us.

"Federales!" someone shouted.

My heart dropped to my stomach when I saw canons being wheeled into position. All pointed toward the city, toward us.

Suddenly, a roar of voices arose as women screamed and cried, picking up their children, running to the bridge. I quickly strapped Luisito to Abuelita's back as she shouted out prayers. Amelia stood frozen, looking at the men on the hill. I scooped her up and carried her away.

We dashed past carts, donkeys, and buggies—anyone moving slower than us. I looked back. Abuelita was slipping behind.

"Hurry," I said and stretched out my arm. She grasped my hand as we continued running.

We dodged children and dogs, trampled cages and broken crates. We came to a sudden stop when we clashed with a wall of people at the start of the bridge.

Abuelita put her hand to her chest. She wheezed and coughed with fury. I rested Amelia over my hip and stretched my neck, trying to find another way.

Abuelita untied her shawl. "Take Luisito," she said between gasps. I put Amelia down and strapped Luisito to my back. I then snatched Amelia's hand.

"Grab Abuelita's hand," I said loudly to Amelia.

"No." Abuelita pushed Amelia's hand away. "You three keep going."

"We're not leaving you behind," I shouted over the cries of women and children.

Amelia wailed.

"*No llores,* m'ija," said Abuelita. "I'll catch up. But leave now, otherwise none of us will make it across."

I hesitated. I was reluctant to leave Abuelita in the hands of the Federales.

"*Orale, vayense!*" Abuelita shouted and shoved us away.

I clutched Amelia's hand and dragged her behind me into the deluge of people. I shoved and elbowed my way through the horde until we stopped only steps from the iron gates. My heartbeat boomed loud in my ears.

Between the heads of people, I caught a glimpse of the American soldiers. Their red faces were as desperate as ours. They knew we were about to be slaughtered.

A small boy clung to the gate and shouted, "*Ayúdenos, por favor!* Help us!" Others prayed out loud and stretched their arms through the gate, pleading for their lives.

A wave of screams reached us, and every head turned to the hills. A cloud of dust traveled downward, toward the city. The Federales were coming for us.

Terror ripped through me. People frantic with fear fought and clawed at each other to reach the gate. A woman across from us pulled at her hair while her child covered his ears and wailed.

"Amelia, grab my waist," I shouted. "Don't let go." I quickly untied my shawl and secured Luisito in front of me. People shoved and pressed us against the railing. I turned my back to the frenzy, trying to shelter Amelia and Luisito.

An American soldier yelled to his comrades and then to us. His voice rang with horror and anguish. As he pressed his hands against his temples, he knocked off his sage-green hat. Unfamiliar words spewed from his mouth, but his face and agitated body told me we were doomed and there was nothing he could do about it.

Luisito clung to my neck, his face turning wildly at every scream. Amelia tightened her grip around my waist. I snugged her head against me, hoping to provide comfort. Below us, el Río Bravo sparkled. Its calm and poised flow contrasted with the storm above it.

Suddenly, the commotion among the American soldiers changed. There were shouts and lots of yelling. I stood on the tips of my toes and saw two American soldiers at a distance. They ran down the bridge toward us, shouting and waving their arms. The soldier with the fallen hat turned to us. The angst in his face had been replaced with haste. He and another soldier pushed back their slung rifles and grabbed the gate. Slowly, the heavy, solid, and impenetrable gate swung open.

I swept Amelia up and carried her and Luisito along with the stream of people. We ran past the iron gates, and a rush of joy shot through me. I laughed and cried at the same time, wanting to hug every American soldier who motioned for us to run through.

With Amelia and Luisito still in my arms, I sprinted up the bridge until my heart, swollen with gratitude, almost burst when we stepped on American soil.

I put Amelia down next to a tall pole and leaned myself against it. I gasped for air and wheezed between coughs, hugging the pole with one arm. The metal felt cold on my face.

I set Luisito down, and he quickly grabbed at my leg to lift himself up.

Sounds of metal clinking, of fabric whipping in the air, turned my gaze upward. Atop the pole waved the flag I'd seen the day before. Sunrays penetrated its red, white, and blue colors, bringing them to life. My heart squeezed with pain and sorrow, wishing Papá and Pablo were here with us.

Amelia's hand clutched the side of my skirt. She kept her eyes fixed on the river of people rushing past us. American soldiers guided carts, donkeys, and people who ran with faces full of fear, as if they'd just slipped through the hands of death.

My eyes darted from person to person and from

face to face, searching franticly for Abuelita. Armed American troops ran past us, downslope, toward the bridge. I caught sight of the gate and saw people cramming through it, trampling those who fell.

Faces grew more anxious, more dreadful. Women atop wagons looked back, crying and shouting out names of loved ones who'd been left behind. Small children wailed, their heads thrown back, and screamed for their mothers who weren't at their sides.

My chest tightened when I looked back to the bridge. On the Mexican side, near the line where the bridge met land, a barricade of about fifty horsemen rushed to break the flow of people. Federales jumped off their horses and grasped at the people trying to flee. They snatched women by their clothes and wrestled men to the ground. Children were grabbed away, forcing their mothers to turn back.

I couldn't tell if Abuelita had made it beyond the wall of Federales. All I could see was the commotion on the Mexican side and the American soldiers beginning to close the gate. The last remaining stragglers who'd evaded the Federales slipped through the shrinking gap. Some fell to their knees, and American soldiers helped them up, ushering them out of the way. Once the dust settled, all that remained was a curtain of khaki uniforms behind a shut gate.

Luisito began to cry, and as he tapped on my leg all I could do was focus on the dwindling number of people staggering toward us. My eyes fixated on an old woman, and I saw what I thought was Abuelita's distinctive waddle. She was the last person to make it through the gate.

My heart, about to rejoice, stopped beating when a man and a boy ran up and embraced her. It wasn't Abuelita.

My body quivered from head to toe. Despite Amelia standing next me and Luisito begging for attention, I could no longer hold myself together. A wicked, ill feeling snaked through me and constricted my insides. It told me, repeatedly, I had failed to keep my promise. I began to sob, and I shook so hard, I had to press my hands against my stomach to keep from doubling over in pain.

"Mira," shouted Amelia. "She's right there!"

I snapped my head to Amelia. She pointed behind us.

"Abuelita!" Amelia ran to a wagon that had stopped a few feet from us.

I blinked twice and saw a man help an old woman climb off the wagon. I blinked again. It was Abuelita. No sooner had she set her feet on the ground than Amelia wrapped her arms around her waist, not letting go. I scooped Luisito up and dashed toward them.

Abuelita's hair was rumpled, and her blouse was torn at the sleeves. Her face, though weary, gave me the most loving smile ever. She cupped my chin with her hands, and gently, I reached over and touched every fresh scratch on her face. Her eyes were red and swollen, but the fire I'd believed to be extinguished burned brighter than ever in them.

I held my family tight as my toes grasped the new land beneath us. I could still smell the desert on all of us, along with the dampness of the last two days. A new smell, however, came to me. It was sweet and welcoming, yet as foreign as the voices around us.

I counted my blessings, one by one. I was alive, with my family, and in America. I was grateful for all those things and for my bare feet too. Thanks to them, I had crossed the desert and outrun the Federales. But most importantly, they had helped me keep my promise to my papá.

twenty-five
TIERRA NUEVA

The last warm rays shined upon us and seeped through the American flag. Hundreds of us, women and children, sat on the ground and huddled under the bright, waving colors. I kept my gaze up, mesmerized, unable to count all of the stars. I could hardly believe we'd made it here. Three years ago, a star had crossed our sky, spreading fear of doom. Today, stars flapped above us, giving us a sense of hope and tranquility.

We sat on the edge of an open field. In the center, men who'd run across the bridge earlier worked alongside American soldiers. Together, they hurriedly set up tents between us and el Río Bravo. Across the river, the Federales guarded the Mexican side, assuring no one else could cross. Beyond that, on the western sky, the sun set calmly on another day.

My soul ached for the people who hadn't made it across. Their fate lay in the hands of the Federales. My thoughts wondered back to Huitzilopochtli, the hummingbird I'd seen earlier. Had that tiny bird distracted me and kept from venturing out to find more food? Had it led me to be closer to the bridge, knowing what was to happen? Maybe there was something to be said for all the omens and signs Abuelita swore by.

Luisito's squealing caught my attention. His short legs wobbled as Amelia walked with him, stooped over, holding his hands. Abuelita, a few steps away, cheered and stretched out her arms, urging Luisito to come to her. It was a relief to see them smile again.

As the cool, autumn breeze blew across the field, I reached into my pocket and pulled out my baby diamond. It felt different in my hand. I inspected it under the sun's orange glow and noticed new ridges and grooves. I was sure I knew every nick and curve in my baby diamond. How could I have missed these marks? How did they even get there?

I thought back to the soldier who had thrown my

rock on the floor as they destroyed our home. I thought about the boulders we'd scraped roughly in the desert as well as the rail I'd dragged myself against on the train bridge. Maybe that's how the new marks had formed? Unable to explain it, I traced each new groove. Some were deep while others were mere scratches. Suddenly, it dawned on me that I too had new marks, but unlike the ones on my rock, I knew how mine had formed.

The desert had scarred the bottoms of my feet, and each struggle we'd endured had etched new grooves in my soul. Mamá's passing, Papá's conscription, the war, the wilderness—all had marked me with sorrow and despair, but also with strength. The deeper indentations, the ones I would cling to for life, had been formed by encounters with formidable people. Adeline had taught me to write my name, and through her noble nature, I'd learned that sincere friendships can sprout even amid the darkest moments and places. Marietta taught me about courage, the type that comes from deep within even in a world that's falling apart. Papá's bravery was also a lesson to me. He'd joined something he detested, all for the sake of his family. Doña Amparo and Luz had taught me the struggle of accepting pain and loss. Both had lost what was most dear to them while pursuing what they believed in. And baby Chencha, in her tenderness, showed me the innocent side of war. Her death, like Mamá's, was a sorrow I'd carry forever, but it'd taught me how beautiful and yet fragile life is. All these marks had shaped me and would continue to shape me for the rest of my days.

I drew in my breath, and emotions as different as the scents of this new country stirred inside me. Some elevated me as high as the moon while others tried to sink me into a dark abyss. The thought of never seeing Papá or Pablo again, especially after having come this far, was unbearable. Someway, somehow, I hoped Papá could find us. I knew I would never see Esperanzas again, at least not the town I'd known since birth. Despite these harsh truths, I was hopeful to one day see Mexico flourish into a country full of peace and prosperity for the people who'd fought and given up so much for her. For now, I was eager to explore this new land, eager to meet its people and welcome new opportunities. Every struggle and challenge I'd grapple with and every failure and victory that lay ahead would dig deep into me and help chisel out my true character.

And I knew then, with all my heart, that one day I would burst with light and shine like the baby diamond I have always longed to be.

THE INSPIRATION FOR BAREFOOT DREAMS OF PETRA LUNA

I am blessed to have grown up listening to stories of my ancestors, especially stories of my grandmother, Güela Pepa, and my great-grandmother, Güelita Juanita. Both women grew up surrounded by harsh poverty and prejudice, but always faced adversity with bold spirits and resilience.

My great-grandmother, Juanita Martínez, inspired the core of *Barefoot Dreams of Petra Luna*. She, along with her family, escaped her burning village in 1913 during the Mexican Revolution. Unlike Petra, my great-grandmother was nine years old when she, her father, two younger siblings, and two cousins crossed the scorching desert by foot and reached the border town of Piedras Negras, Coahuila. At the border, their entry into the United States was denied along with hundreds of other refugees.

As a child, I sat mesmerized, listening to my great-grandmother recount the moment she and her family learned that the Federales were on their way to attack the town. "Los Federales were evil," she'd say. "We knew they'd slaughter us." According to her, hundreds of people flocked to the international bridge and pleaded to the American soldiers to open the gates. The situation worsened when the rush of mounted Federales approached the town's small hills. My great-grandmother, despite the many decades having passed since that event, always recalled the fright in her father's eyes. "Then suddenly," my great-grandmother would say with nostalgic surprise, "the gates swung open." As she spoke, the joy and relief she'd experienced that day always came to life, making me feel as if I too had run across that bridge. At the end, she'd always remind us of her immense gratitude to the United States for having given her refuge.

I had always wondered about the validity of my great-grandmother's story. I wondered if some of the details had been stretched to give her story an edge. Had that many people, really all at once, rushed to the bridge? Had my great-grandmother and her family been that close to death? While contemplating writing a children's article about it, I embarked on a research journey to find out the facts. Not having an exact date, I searched through books on the Mexican Revolution and US-Mexican migration but found nothing. I began sorting through four major Texas newspapers beginning with the year 1910. After months of research, I found an article that described my great-grandmother's story. The event occurred in the early afternoon of October 6, 1913, and it wasn't hundreds of people who'd tried to flee across like she'd stated, it was thousands. Over six thousand, to be exact. Everything else—the desperation, the pleading, and the rage of the Federales—was exactly as she'd recounted it.

Working on this book has fulfilled me in many ways, and despite my grandmother and great-grandmother no longer living, I feel closer to them than ever. Thanks to them and my mother, I learned stories that I would have never learned from books or school. Unfortunately, many stories like my great-grandmother's or like Petra's remain in the shadows. How do we fix this? I believe we fix it with curiosity. We need to be curious. We need to look to our ancestors and ask questions. We need to listen to their stories, write them down, on paper or on our hearts, and pass them on. By doing this, we bring stories of bravery, of humanity, and of great compassion to the light and, in turn, we learn more about ourselves and keep the bold spirits of our ancestors alive.

Alda P. Dobbs

Conroe, Texas

October 27, 2020

Timeline

1910

//

MAY 1910 Halley's Comet looms over the skies. Many in Mexico view it as a bad omen.

JUNE 1910 Mexico holds elections and President Porfirio Díaz declares himself president for a seventh term. He has his opponent, Francisco Madero, arrested.

AUGUST 1910 Tensions rise as numerous protests erupt and are quickly crushed by soldiers and police. Newspapers are shut down and journalists are arrested.

SEPTEMBER 1910 Mexico celebrates its one hundredth Anniversary of Independence, as well as

President Porfirio Díaz's eightieth birthday with elegant balls and parades.

OCTOBER 1910 Madero flees to San Antonio, Texas, where he drafts his "Plan of San Luis Potosí," declaring President Díaz's reelection fraudulent and urging Mexicans to take up arms against him.

NOVEMBER 20, 1910 According to the "Plan of San Luis Potosí," this day at 1800 hours (6:00 p.m.) is the official start of the Mexican Revolution.

DECEMBER 1910 Miners, ranchers, peasants, schoolteachers, lawyers, merchants, and women join the revolution.

1911

APRIL 1911 The revolution becomes more organized as battles are won against federal forces and more regions are being controlled by the Revolucionarios, the rebels.

MAY 1911 The leader of the northern rebel forces, General Francisco "Pancho" Villa, wins a major battle at Ciudad Juárez, and after thirty-one years of dictatorship, President Díaz steps down. He is quickly exiled to France.

NOVEMBER 1911 Francisco Madero is elected president, taking 90 percent of the votes, and the leader of the revolutionary forces in southern Mexico, Emiliano Zapata, writes the "Plan of Ayala," demanding land reform.

1912

MARCH 1912 Two powerful families in Mexico fear President Madero will implement land reform. They supply money and weapons to Pascual Orozco, a onetime ally of Pancho Villa, and promise him political power in return for fighting against Madero.

APRIL 1912 To put down Orozco's rebellion, President Madero turns to a former general of the Díaz regime, General Victoriano Huerta.

OCTOBER 1912 General Huerta defeats Orozco's rebellion, but a new rebellion, led by Porfirio Díaz's nephew, Félix Díaz, emerges.

1913

//

FEBRUARY 1913 General Huerta and Félix Díaz secretly negotiate a coup against President Madero, and with the "blessing" of U.S. Ambassador Henry Lane Wilson, Madero is arrested. Three days later, Madero, his brother, and his vice president are executed.

MARCH 1913 After General Huerta takes office, he ships Félix Díaz to Japan, silences the press, jails 110 members of congress, and has over one hundred of Madero's supporters shot. In the U.S., President Woodrow Wilson takes the oath of office.

APRIL 1913 General Huerta and his Federales fight Pancho Villa and Venustiano Carranza in northern Mexico and Emiliano Zapata in the south.

SEPTEMBER 27, 1913 More than three thousand refugees head north toward the border town of Piedras Negras, Coahuila, following raids, forced conscriptions, and destruction of the region's towns and villages.

SEPTEMBER 28, 1913 A regiment of 1,600 Federales heads to Piedras Negras to control the northern border.

SEPTEMBER 30, 1913 U.S. Cavalry and Field Artillery soldiers and a hospital unit from Fort Sam Houston in San Antonio are ordered to the border town of Eagle Pass, Texas.

OCTOBER 2, 1913· A storm system develops in the area, bringing floods to central Texas and heavy downpours at the border. After cases of smallpox are detected, two hundred refugees who had crossed into the U.S. are returned to Mexico.

OCTOBER 3, 1913· A head tax of five dollars is imposed for Mexicans wanting to cross into the U.S. As rebels begin to leave Piedras Negras, they destroy bridges and mines.

OCTOBER 4, 1913· A band of women soldiers, belonging to the advanced guard of the Federales, rides through the outskirts of Piedras Negras. They announce the approach of the federal regiment and threaten people with death if they join the rebels or attempt to cross into the U.S.

OCTOBER 5, 1913˙ Colonel Francisco Sánchez Herrera of the revolutionary forces assembles the refugees in the town square of Piedras Negras and pleads with them to remain loyal to the rebel cause and promises that federal rule will be short-lived.

OCTOBER 6, 1913˙ (IN THE TWILIGHT HOURS) The last of the remaining rebels leave the military barracks at Piedras Negras.

OCTOBER 6, 1913˙ The Federales arrive at the hilltops of Piedras Negras, and more than six thousand refugees flock to the international bridge. As federal cavalry troops rush toward the border, U.S. Army soldiers open the bridge.

* May have occurred the day before or after. Different newspaper sources and books report the events happening on different days. The discrepancies may be due to the remote location of the border and the ongoing conflict in Mexico.

Acknowledgments

I want to start by giving my most heartfelt thanks to my mother, Lorena Chapa, for the many family stories she shared with me, for instilling pride in my culture and my ancestors, and for teaching me Spanish in a time when bilingualism was looked down upon. I also want to thank my great-grandmother, Güelita Juanita, and my grandmother, Güela Pepa, for their bold spirits and determination to push their families further down the path of opportunity. Their stories are the heart and soul of this book.

It takes a village to raise a child, and I believe the same applies when writing a book. During my initial research, much help came from incredible librarians like Tim Blevins at the Pikes Peak Library System, Susan Dognaux at the Louisville Free Public Library, and Noël Cammack at the Montgomery County Memorial Library. I am forever grateful. A special thanks to the great staff at the Texana/Genealogy Department in the San Antonio Public Library and to Carlos Cortéz at the University of Texas at San Antonio Special Collections for their guidance in researching the Mexican Revolution.

I am grateful to the brave journalists like John Reed, whose interviews with rebels during the Mexican Revolution inspired the sentiments of Marietta and other characters in my book. The works of anthropologist Oscar Lewis and Friedrich Katz and historians Elizabeth Salas, Ernesto Galarza, Alan Knight, Andrés Reséndez Fuentes, Esther R. Perez, Nina Kallas, Linda B. Hall, and Don M. Coerver provided me with accurate accounts and narratives that inspired characters and settings.

I'm enormously indebted to the many organizations that contributed to my growth as a writer: The Writing Roosters, The Highlights Foundation, The Sustainable Arts Foundation, Kid's Book Revisions, Denise Vega's Believe Scholarship, the Barbara Deming Memorial Fund, the Dorothy Markinko Scholarship with the Rutgers University Council on Children's Literature,

We Need Diverse Books, and the scholarships and mentorship programs provided by various SCBWI chapters, including Rocky Mountain, Brazos Valley, Houston, and Austin. Many thanks to my two mentors and fellow authors, Jeannie Mobley and Joy Preble, for their excellent feedback on my work. Also, to Heila Rogers for her input on my early drafts. I will always be grateful to all of you.

I want to thank my fantastic agent, Joan Paquette, for seeing potential in my work long before it was complete. Because of her efforts, I was lucky to be paired with my brilliant editor, Molly Cusick. Thank you, Molly, for your enthusiasm and amazing insight, and for encouraging me to take Petra's story to the next level. An enormous thanks to all the wonderful people at Sourcebooks who helped bring this book to life and connect it to readers, including Jordan Kost, Maryn Arreguín, and Michelle Mayhall in the art department; Heather Moore, Ashlyn Keil, Valerie Pierce, Tiffany Schulz, Jenna Quatraro, Amanda Farrell, Viridiana Contreras, Lizzie Lewandowski, Katie Stutz, Katia Herrera in marketing and publicity; and production editor Cassie Gutman. Also, a big thanks to the amazing cover artist John Jay Cabuay, and to Manuela Velasco for their insightful copyedits. Thank you all for your dedication and for believing in my book.

A special thanks to my friend, beta reader, and talented writer, Laura Reseau, for her encouragement and for being a beacon of light in this sometimes-nebulous industry. To my friends and family who never grew tired of asking and hearing about my book, and to Tom and Pat Dobbs for all their support. To my sisters Arianné, Adriana, and Laura who's charm and innocence as little girls inspired the character of Amelia.

Finally, my deepest gratitude to my two kids, Annabella and Nate. Your love gives me the fortitude to never give up. Thank you for your understanding and for always showing excitement when I share writing ideas, no matter how wild they are. And lastly, I want to thank the person who suggested I start writing in the first place—my husband and best friend, Mike Dobbs. Mike read countless drafts, brainstormed with me, cooked, cleaned, and took care of everything when I had to shut myself away to write. Thank you for pushing me to keep going even when I thought I couldn't. Gracias por todo, amor.

About the Author

Alda P. Dobbs has won various writing awards including the Barbara Deming Memorial Fund Award and the Sustainable Arts Foundation Grant. *Barefoot Dreams of Petra Luna* is drawn from experiences Alda's great-grandmother endured during the Mexican Revolution in 1913. Alda was born in a small town in northern Mexico and moved to San Antonio, Texas, as a child. She studied physics and worked as an engineer before pursuing her love of storytelling. She is as passionate about connecting children to their past, their communities, different cultures, and nature as she is about writing.

Alda lives with her husband and two children outside Houston, Texas. To learn more about her, visit aldapdobbs.com.

PETRA'S JOURNEY CONTINUES IN

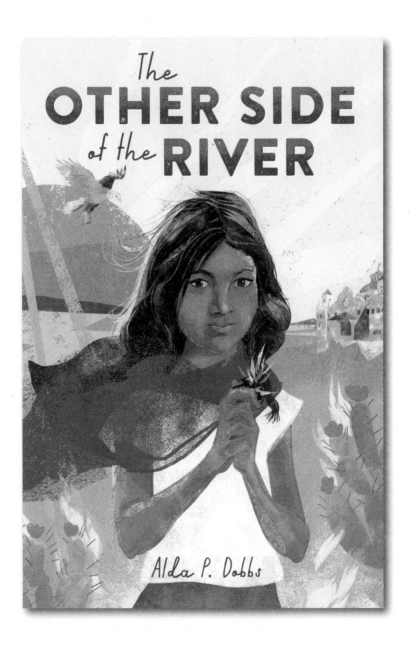

The
OTHER SIDE
of the RIVER

Alda P. Dobbs